MONTY
AND THE
MONSTER

ISBN: 978-0-9984492-3-4

Cover design by www.ebooklaunch.com
Chapter illustrations by Kev Hopgood

Rhonda Smiley

Dedicated to Robert Brousseau,
whose imaginings were the inspiration for this book

CHAPTER 1

Move, butt-wipe."

That's Kyle, my older brother, trying to shove me out of the way with the door of the U-Haul so he can get out. Normally, I'd fight back with some name-calling of my own, but I'm paralyzed with disgust as I stand before the ugliest house I've ever seen. And there's so much of it too. Three stories—four if you count the attic—of peeling paint, dangling shutters, and boarded-up windows. A forest of weeds taller than me has burgeoned from the cracks in the front walkway, and I wonder if anyone thought to pack a machete.

Kyle manages to knock me aside with the door and exits the truck. He towers a foot over me. More than our six-year difference should allow if you ask me. It's not that I'm jealous (much), it's that I'm almost thirteen. Shouldn't I be taller by now?

He unties my magician's cape, and it falls off, hitting the ground before I realize what's happening.

"Kyle!" It's real satin and not easy to keep clean. I snatch it up, wipe it off, and put it back on.

Dad jumps out of the driver's side and inhales deeply as he steps between Kyle and me. He puts his arms around us like we're all in this together even though I had nothing to do with it. With a beaming smile, he says, "Does this house have character or what?"

"What," Kyle and I say at the same time.

Dad bounds up the wobbly steps of the porch and disappears inside. I fear for his life, but Kyle follows him in so I figure there's safety in numbers.

Resigned to having no vote in my own life, I try to coax Watson out of the front seat. He's the basset hound I've had for five years and three houses, not including this one. He didn't do anything to deserve this, but no one gets to choose their family, and he's stuck with us.

"C'mon, Watson. You live here too."

Watson scuttles back in protest. "Right. Why should you listen to me? I'm only the guy who picks up your poop."

He stares at me, steadfast, but I'm not in the mood to argue over who's boss. I half drag, half lift the bundle of fur and slobber off the seat and deposit him on the ground. "You're welcome."

Watson sticks to me like Velcro now as I go to the back of the truck and raise the cargo door. Cardboard boxes identified by the Sharpie labeling system take up most of the trailer. Our beds take up the rest. As far as our other furniture, Dad leaves that to the professionals. Hopefully they won't be a week late like the last time we moved. I hop in, but Watson can't make the jump and watches from outside with his paws on the bumper.

I climb over the boxes, ignoring the "fragile" or "handle with care" warnings because Dad put something similar on every box, regardless of its contents. Wedged between "utensils" and "home movies" is what I'm looking for: my favorite skateboard.

I pry it loose and hop out of the truck.

Skateboard under my arm and Watson on my heels, I trudge up the steps. The front door has glass panels on top, but you'd never know from the street—that's how dirty they are.

I swing the door wide open, and a repulsive smell like sweaty toe jam hits me, hits me hard. My insides revolt, threatening to unleash two Twinkies and a bag of Twizzlers projectile-style, but I'm able to stop the mutiny. Closing off the part of my esophagus that leads to the back door of my nose, I become a mouth breather so I can enter without puking.

I stay by the front door and take it all in. The main floor is huge. Like mansion-huge. If it wasn't a dump, I'd think we were rich, but even the cobwebs have cobwebs. To my right, against the wall, a staircase leads up to the second and third floors. Off the landing, or "foyer" as Dad calls these things, a living room goes on forever until it becomes the dining room, where a brass chandelier hangs from a rusty chain over nothing, which is good since most of the links are coming apart.

With no furniture, curtains, or rugs, I'm afraid to guess what the stench is from. At least Dad's removing boards from some of the broken windows to allow a cleansing breeze in. And on the bright side, the wood floors have nicks and scratches all over so Watson won't have to worry about ruining them (like he worries about anything other than food, walks, and licking his privates).

I sail off the landing on my board, pulling a sweet 360, and Dad gives me one of his disapproving looks.

"Monty, what did I say about skateboarding in the house?"

"I thought that was only when we lived in nice houses."

Kyle laughs. "Burn!"

"Monty—" Dad starts with his sympathetic posture, but I cut him off.

"What? It's not like I'm gonna trash the floors. Look at 'em."

He sighs, and I know I hurt his feelings, but I can't take another one of his chats. I wish people would stop writing books telling parents how to talk to their kids.

"Let's get the boxes," he says.

Grumbling, I turn to exit and find myself in the face of a wonky-eyed old man. *Agh.* I stumble back. The man bypasses me, unfazed, and pulls Dad in for a kiss—wet, sloshy contact— left cheek, right cheek, left cheek. Kyle glances over with his best *yikes!* look, and Watson growls but from the safety of the dining room.

"Robert!" the ancient says. "Robert, Robbie, Rob." He actually tears up. "Doctor Robert Hyde. Look at you!" He pulls Dad in for another kiss, but Dad extricates himself with a smile. Still, the guy stays nose to nose with him.

"It's good to see you, Doctor Petrovic," Dad says.

So this is Dad's new boss. His old college professor. Dr. Petrovic. He looks more like a mad scientist with his nest of stringy grey hair, long bushy beard, stained lab coat, and army boots.

"We are close, Robert. Very, very close."

I'll say. They'd be married in some states.

"You had a good trip? You're rested? You'll be in class tomorrow? Will you be in class tomorrow, Robert? I don't have all day. Answer me."

"Yes. I'll be there."

The doctor lets out a sigh that smells like pastrami, and for the second time in one day, I find myself fighting vomit convulsions—not a good omen—but a woman's voice sends everything back down.

"Hi, Robert."

It's the way she said it. *Hi, Robert.* Like she's his girlfriend or something. *Hi, Robert, tee hee.* Sickening.

Disheveled and harried, same as the doctor, she's also wearing a lab coat with stains on it. Her hair's in a messy ponytail with curly strands escaping every which way. But she's pretty. Really pretty for someone as old as Dad. I look over to him, and he's all goo-goo eyed.

"Ashanta," he says with the same chumminess she used, and throws his arms around her in a warm hug.

My turn to glance at Kyle, but he grins this time. My best recourse is to roll my eyes. I'm agitated, and I don't even know why.

"What're you doing here?" Dad asks.

"Didn't Doctor Petrovic tell you? I'm his associate professor."

The doctor yanks her with him as he makes for the exit like a bank robber. "See you in class tomorrow, Robbie-Bobbie-Boo. You said so."

They're out the door in a flash but not before Ashanta looks over her shoulder at Dad. He waves with a giggle. A giggle! From a grown man.

"Who's that?" I get right to the point. Arms crossed, resting on the tail of my board with the nose up, to show how serious I am.

"That's my new boss, Doctor Petrovic," Dad says.

I glare at him, reminding him I'm not the jock in the family.

"Oh, you mean her? She's an old college friend."

"With benefits?" Kyle asks.

"Don't be crude," Dad says, then turns to me. "Say, why don't you take a tour of the university with Kyle later? Maybe you'll go to my old alma mater too."

Nice deflection. "As if."

Kyle stomps on the nose of my board, throwing me off. "You know, you have to actually go outside to make friends, Monty.

The house doesn't come with them."

"Whatever." I pop my board up, tucking it under my arm. Because I'm cool like that.

"Whatever," Kyle mocks, reminding me I'm not cool like that.

"Quit it," I retort.

"Quit it," he says.

"Shut up."

"Shut up."

"Dad!"

"Dad!"

"Kyle . . ." Dad says, too little too late. I'm already out the door.

"What? Got him out of the house, didn't I?" Kyle says. I hear them through the broken windows.

"Monty doesn't adjust as well as you do. You're supposed to help him."

"Dad, helping Monty is a full-time job."

Nice. I jump onto my board, grab my helmet from the back of the U-Haul, and skate off. I hate this place. Hate it even more than the last one.

# CHAPTER 2

I wasn't lying when I said I didn't want to tour Clear Rock University.

But when your neighborhood is basically campus, it's hard not to get the tour once you go outside. All the houses in this gated community, nicknamed Crampus, are owned by the university and are for faculty and their families, ours included. Dad says the nickname is short for Clear Rock Campus, but I think it's because you feel crammed into a neighborhood.

The houses span a square mile or so, starting at the main entrance. Past the houses, closer to the school, are the dorms for students whose families are lucky enough to not work here. And past those, taking up half the neighborhood, are the ivy-covered brick buildings of Clear Rock U: Administration, Fine Arts, Liberal Arts, Business and Law, Library, and Science. Dad pitched it with such joy, you'd have thought we were moving to Disneyland. Me, I'd rather eat brussels sprouts than live here. All school all the time? That's just cruel.

A car honks behind me, annoyed I'm skating in the street, so I pop an ollie onto the sidewalk, not wanting to make enemies.

I pass some guys playing football on one of the front lawns, and we exchange glances. I'm pretty sure they're around my age, but they don't say anything to me. When I get to the end of the block, I circle back, determined to introduce myself—*who's making friends now, Kyle?*—but I chicken out and keep going.

One of them says, "Weirdo," and they all laugh. Whatever. I don't play football anyway.

I weave through the neighborhood, on the verge of self-pity, when I'm halted by that familiar sound.

Wheels on cement.

At the end of the street, two teens on their boards catch air off the curb and keep going. No way! Last place we lived, nobody skated. I keep pace without getting too close to them. Maybe half a block behind.

They skate toward the Science building, but they're too young to be in college so I keep following. Students (who for some reason are compelled to go to the library on the weekend) skirt out of the way of the two skaters even though signs forbid skateboards, rollerblades, and bicycles on the walkway. I don't get the same respect and nearly wipe out when a square-headed troll pulls a fake lunge to intimidate me. My board gets away, but I'm still on my feet, and I chase after and hop back on.

The walkway branches off to the left, going around the Science building, which is where the skaters go. As I circle the building to follow, I'm awestruck. Hidden behind the academia is a real-life Xanadu. A skate park!

It's past the playground and picnic areas, softball and soccer fields, tennis and basketball courts. Forgoing the path, I pop up my board and sprint across the grass in a beeline. I can't get there fast enough. As I catch my breath outside the gate, the awesomeness drenches me like Splash Mountain. A bowl, hips, curbs, spines, ramp, and a full pipe spilling in from the snake run. It's teeming with skaters, mostly guys, but a few girls too. Some of the thrashers are good, but not as good as me.

I round the gate until I find the entrance and go in. Skaters look my way briefly, a few with smirks, before turning back to their tricks. Playing it cool, I saunter to the bowl and wait for an opening. Etiquette first.

When it's clear, I drop in, carving the bowl nice and easy to get a feel for it. The surface is smooth, not like the pool on the foreclosure property I used to sneak onto back in Ohio (two houses ago). Skating is my comfort zone, even with a bunch of strangers, and I'm happy for the first time since we piled into the U-Haul.

Most of the skaters do simple grabs and stalls, and I do the same for a few runs, to fit in. No one's saying anything to me yet, no nods or hellos, but I still get a sideways glance here and there. In an attempt to spark some interaction, I amp up my game. Sailing majestically off the lip, I nail a 180 before landing flawlessly in the bowl. As I exit on the other side, I catch my board midair—no big deal—and casually turn to get some recognition. But no one's looking at me because they're busy crowding this hotshot who enters doing a Caballerial kickflip like it's nothing.

Typical. No matter where we move, there's always one of those. The type where everything comes easy for him, even his stupid good looks. For once I'd like to be the popular guy in the room.

I'm so inside my head I don't realize I'm staring directly at a girl until she says, "What're you gawking at, Dracula?"

I snap to—*Dracula? I'm a magician, not a vampire*—but I pretend I don't hear her and drop in, carving the bowl, no tricks. My insides beg to look back, but I don't have the nerve. I'm pretty sure she's cute and that her eyes are brown because the first thing I thought of was Whoppers. Big round Whoppers.

Ignoring the boisterous crowd, I do my own thing, but the popular guy drops in intentionally too close to me. I spin to avoid a collision and—*crud monkeys!* My board flies out from under me, and I hit the wall in only the most awkward position known to man before sliding to the bottom.

"He eats it," the cute girl says, laughing. I get a good look at her now. She has long black hair, pulled back in a ponytail, caramel-colored skin, and a mouth full of perfect teeth. I can see them all due to her laughter.

"Yeahno!" screams Mr. Popular because he isn't getting enough attention.

My face is on fire. Redder than Mars. Since I'm not lucky enough to be struck by lightning, I pretend to think it's funny too and chuckle as I get to my feet.

"The poser's laughing at himself," says Mr. Popular, and the others laugh harder.

I grab my board and climb out of the bowl.

Skating home on the fumes of indignation, I arrive to more bad news.

Dad's unloading the U-Haul and thinks I'm just in time. He tries to hand me two boxes: "tablecloths" and "kitchen towels." Both, apparently, are fragile and need to be handled with care.

"Here, take these to the kitchen," he says.

"Where's Kyle?"

"He put in his time, if that's what you're getting at. He even unpacked his room."

"So he got to pick his room first?"

"Don't worry, Monty, there are plenty to choose from."

"Yeah, but he always gets what he wants."

"You weren't here."

"Whose fault is that?"

"Monty, can we do this later please? We have a lot of work to do."

"Can't I help after I pick my room?"

"Fine," he says in a rare bout of reasonableness.

I jet into the house and up the stairs. Watson chases me, thinking it's a game. The second floor has three doors in the hallway ahead of me and one behind me. I check out the room behind me first.

Kyle's. And I'd hardly say it's unpacked, but whatever.

It's at the front of the house with windows that curve in a semicircle, giving you a view up and down the street. But if I know Kyle, he didn't pick this room for its view. It also has a small balcony, perfect for sneaking in and out of the house. He might be Dad's favorite, but he still has a curfew.

I check out the other rooms down the hall. A bathroom and two small bedrooms. Nothing speaks to me. Or Watson. We go to the third floor. Three more doors. One leads to the master, twice the size of any of the rooms on the second floor. Dad's got dibs, judging by the stack of boxes. Across from the master is the bathroom, also huge. The room at the front of the house, above Kyle's, is tiny and doesn't have a balcony for sneaking in and out. I'm about to retreat to the second floor to pick a room, but Watson sniffs his way to the end of the hall, drawing my attention to a nook I didn't notice before.

It's the entry to a walled-in staircase going up. At the top is a closed door. Must be the attic. I try to urge Watson up first, but he melts into a blob. I step over him and climb to the top, stairs creaking the entire time. Half hoping the door is locked,

I test the handle. It turns. *Here goes nothing.* I push open the door.

Rank and grungy, it's the attic, all right. Rafters on the ceiling are home to a myriad of webs dotted with dead flies, but the walls are finished and so are the floors, which are wide planks of wood beneath an inch of dust. One large window on the far wall opposite the door is the only source of light cutting through the spooky darkness. *Cool.*

I found my room.

CHAPTER 3

Sitting on the bottom porch step, I roll my board under my feet as Watson lies on top of it.

It's our version of "Rock-a-bye Baby"; I just have to make sure I don't run over his ears. Claiming the attic was sweeter before I had to carry all my stuff up there but totally worth it to see Dad's face when I told him. Now I'm feeling extra sticky and I might smell.

Hard to believe we got here this morning.

Down the block, kids laugh and goof off. The kind of stuff that makes no sense to outsiders. I can't tell if Mr. Popular is there, but I decide he's grounded the rest of the day for being a dipwad. Speaking of—being popular, not being a dipwad—Kyle's across the street, kicked back on the neighbor's porch, enthralling a group of new friends with a story. That's Kyle. Star athlete, outgoing, good-looking. I mean, come on! We're from the same DNA.

He gets up to say his goodbyes, and moans of disappointment run through the crowd. Moans. Of disappointment.

"This place sucks," I say when he's in earshot. He's carrying a bag from Fifi's Boutique, and I don't question it. Whatever Kyle does seems right.

"You always say that."

"Maybe if we didn't move every two months."

"What do you want Dad to do, Monty? Give up good opportunities because you can't make friends?"

"I can make friends. They're just dorks here, that's all."

"Then you should fit right in," he says, swatting my cape so it flies over my head and covers my face.

"Ha ha." I dig myself out, but Kyle's up the steps and in the house in two easy bounds. So much for forming an alliance against Dad.

I drag myself inside, prompting Watson to follow. Curtains are up (over repaired windows), and furniture is in place (thanks to the movers getting here on time), and it looks like a real house. Based on the unappetizing odor coming from the kitchen, Dad's tackling dinner. He thinks giving us McDonald's or pizza is a form of neglect, but I don't get how he can read all these books on raising kids and not understand us at all. Nobody likes tuna casserole.

Nearing the second floor, I hear Kyle in his room jabbering on the phone. His words poke me in my chest, my gut, my forehead, like bullies reminding me how unpopular I am. I quicken my pace to the third floor, then run to the end of the hall and race up to the attic. Only when I enter my room do I feel at home.

Lucky, even.

I have a clear path to the window without having to go around the foot of my bed, which has its headboard up against the wall on the right. Meaning my room is big. In fact, you can't see my bed from the doorway unless you open the door all the way.

Aside from sheets and blankets, I haven't unpacked a

whole lot. Just the important stuff. Like my magic stand. It's actually an old stereo cabinet Mom bought for me at a garage sale. The top hinges up on the right side for when you want to play records, except we removed the turntable so I could use that compartment while performing tricks. It also has shelves underneath to store my props. The whole thing is covered in a black velvet cloth that Mom constructed in a way that the lid could still open and close. I set it up on the other side of the room, between the bed and the window. On the door side, I keep my skateboards. Four in all.

A picture of me, Kyle, and Mom is on the floor, leaning against the wall right next to my bed. It's in one of those plastic frames where you slide the picture in, and the bottom is broken off because that's what happens to cheap plastic when you pack and unpack it fifty times in two years. It's my favorite picture. We're at the zoo, and Mom and I are wearing our top hats and magician capes, and Kyle's rolling his eyes at us.

My dresser and desk are pushed up against the wall opposite the foot of my bed, and the rest of my belongings, boxes and boxes of them, take up the left corner. You never know how much junk you have until you have to bring it somewhere else. Most of the boxes are opened—in other words, accessible enough without having to put things in their proper places— and one of them looks like a volcano spewing lava in the form of clothes.

Taking my position behind the magic stand, I don the all-important top hat and grab my wand. It's showtime.

"As you can see, this is an ordinary wand," I say to Watson. He sniffs it and seems satisfied. "Abracadabra. Kalamazoo. Roses are red, and your butt smells like poo!" I wave the wand dramatically and . . .

Nothing.

"Oh, come on." I fiddle with it, tap it on the magic stand, curse at it, but those flowers aren't making an appearance anytime soon. I toss the piece of crap aside and duck under the black velvet cloth to gather a *Popular Science* magazine and a carton of soy milk. When I surface, Watson is waggling before me with the wand in his mouth, except now it's a bouquet of flowers.

I glare at him. "Nobody likes a show-off, Watson."

He disagrees and lies down with the wand still firmly between his teeth.

Moving on, I flutter the pages of *Popular Science*. "As you can see, this is a boring old magazine. And this is regular old milk." I take a sip from the carton to prove it. "I'm going to make the milk disappear before your eyes. And no, not by drinking it." I wait a beat because I know that would get a laugh if people were here.

With the magazine rolled into a cone, I pour the milk in with confidence—I've done it a million times—but this time it leaks out the bottom. Instinctively, I try to catch it, and lose my grip on the whole container. It hits the floor, smashing open, and splatters everywhere. "Aw, man."

Watson drops the bouquet in favor of lapping up the spilled milk, and I allow it because he's doing me a favor. But then I notice the liquid is seeping into some cracks in the floorboards.

Must investigate.

I push Watson away and note a very specific pattern.

Square.

Like a trapdoor.

On my bedroom floor.

CHAPTER 4

There's no handle on the trapdoor.

I rummage through my "cables and stuff" box in search of a screwdriver and come up with a metal ruler. Good enough. I pry at the square plank until it pops up an inch or two. A dark plume of smoke spills out accompanied by an eggy stench that sends Watson scurrying under my bed.

"Whoo!" And I thought Dad's tuna casserole was bad.

Using my legs, I push the heavy plank until it slides out of position. Sure enough, it's an opening. To somewhere. Three feet by three feet. It's dark in there. Pitch black. I race back to my boxes, this time in search of a flashlight, and find one.

I shine the beam into the abyss and bats shoot out. Fluttering. Screeching. Assaulting. I stumble back, landing on my butt, and cover my head as they circle the room in a frenzy. Watson barks and jumps at them until they find the open window. To be honest, I'm not sure if he was being protective or playful.

Prudently this time, I lean over the opening as I shine the light in. I gasp so loudly, Watson comes scrambling to my rescue, but he misunderstands. Things just got good.

A thick rope ladder leads down.

Waaaaay down.

"I'm going in."

Watson tries to talk me out of it, but I ignore his whining, pocket the flashlight, and slide over the edge until my foot finds the first rung. The ladder sways under my weight. Totally unsteady. I'm still going in. Sixty-eight rungs later—I counted—I reach bottom. When I look up, Watson begs me to return.

"Don't worry, I'll be back."

The narrow passageway hangs a sharp left ten steps in, eliminating any trace of my room, and my shoes become cement blocks. It's not that I think there's an ax-wielding murderer down here, but I don't not think it either. Nonetheless, I proceed, swinging the beam from my flashlight like a lightsaber.

The passage is a maze, and it's not long before I have no idea how far I've gone or which way I'm facing, whether I'm heading back to the ladder or under the property a block over. After the longest few minutes of my life, I reach the end.

Dead end, that is.

"Bogus."

Who builds a tunnel to nowhere?

Irritated, I about-face to stomp my way back, and my foot slips through some metal slats in the floor. Not just my foot. My whole leg sinks through, and I hit the ground with a thud, losing my flashlight in the process. It rolls out of reach, shining a beam on the wall, but I'm more concerned with what I put in motion. I wince, waiting for spikes to drop from the ceiling or a boulder to squash me. But nothing else happens.

Trapped, leg snared between two bars, I brush aside a thick layer of dirt around me and uncover a huge metal grating on the ground. My leg is dangling through the bars of the grating, but I can't see anything below it. Is it a sewer? A subway? A moat of crocodiles waiting to feast? Forgetting the ax-wielding murderer, except for that thought right there, I brush away more dirt until I expose the entire grate. It's as wide as the passageway, about three feet square. Gnarly, but not where I want to die. I wriggle back, yanking and twisting, trying to free my leg. I'm almost out when—*crickets!*—my foot releases, but my Vans sneaker falls into the unknown below.

Unfettered, I grab my flashlight and shine it through the grating. I see it—my brand-new sneaker that cost me five weeks of mowing lawns and doing household chores that Dad said other kids do for free. As if.

Belly down, I reach through the bars but can't . . . quite . . . make it. Suddenly, the grating drops open from one side with me still on it. *Aaaaaaggggghhhhh. Trap. It's a trap!*

I hug the bars, terrified, as the grating unfolds like a Slinky going down stairs, flipping me upside down, right side up, then upside down again until . . . *WHOMP.*

I'm reunited with my shoe. Sort of.

It's next to my head, but I'm still clinging onto the bars. Upside down. Frozen. I listen for heavy breathing or snarling. I hear none of that. In fact, it's eerily quiet, which is almost as bad. Surprised I'm still grasping my flashlight, I make use of it. The beam of light confirms that the space is huge, the size of the entire first floor of the house. There's stuff everywhere, piled high and wide, but no sign of life (more specifically, ax-wielding maniacs or, worse, snakes), so I release my grip from the bars and slither to the floor. First things first. My hard-earned shoe goes back on my foot.

Leading with my flashlight, I tiptoe farther into the buried treasure beneath my house. My room.

There are boxes and barrels and steamer trunks filled with

all kinds of valuables, I imagine, but I resist tearing anything open until I can assess what's before me. A cleared path winds through the room, and I let it be my guide, taking me past furniture and clothing and knickknacks and appliances until I'm stopped by three ginormous wooden crates.

Important-looking crates.

Five feet wide and high with big bold warnings stamped across them. The letters are faded, some entirely, but the message is clear.

OXIC

POI ONOUS

VOLATI E

My cheeks hurt from smiling. *Awesome sauce.*

A rattling noise jolts me back to the ax-wielding maniac, and I throw my hands up in surrender. "I won't tell," I say for some reason. Probably my training as Kyle's younger brother.

More rattling pulls my eye to the source, which is above the important-looking crates. Cellar doors. Jostling in the wind. I flash my light around and see steps leading up to those doors. Two entries to this place. One from my bedroom and one from outside. *Good to know.*

Calmed, I continue my exploration. Next to the crates are two metal tables, the kind Dad has in his labs, and on one of them is a corrugated box sealed with a sticker that reads "equipment." Science equipment, no doubt.

On the floor, next to the table, is a stack of unlabeled boxes. I rip them open, one after the other. Files, files, and more files. *Area 51 Specimen Results. Loch Ness Yeti. Hippocentaur. Early Stage Embryo Test. Project X. Grandma's Recipe for Chicken Poodle Soup.* I hope that last one is a typo.

The final box contains a single item: a big fat leather notebook. Must be a hundred years old. The cover is worn out, and the pages are crinkled, the way paper gets when it gets wet and then dries.

My fingers catch on the cracked hide as I wipe away the dust, and I feel words engraved into it. Same color as the leather, it's hard to read, but it looks like it says *Human Replication and Reanimation.*

Human Replication and Reanimation?

Stunned, I stare at it, heart pounding, and let it sink in real good. Because I know what comes next.

I'm going to *make* a friend. From scratch.

CHAPTER 5

I tear the sticker off the corrugated box of equipment.

It's filled with test tubes, beakers, and petri dishes stained with gunk as if they were packed up in a hurry. Digging farther, I find a microscope, Bunsen burner, forceps, tongs, goggles, pipets, and stirring rods. I organize everything to the best of my knowledge. Petri dishes by the microscope. Beakers by the Bunsen burner. I even have a tray for the tools and a rack to put the test tubes in.

Making a friend might sound preposterous, but they clone sheep and grow ears on mice's backs and put dead people's organs in living people. I bet there was a time when all that seemed impossible.

Beneath the harsh glow of a bare bulb hanging over the metal tables, I open the big fat leather notebook to get cracking.

I should've known. Gibberish. Or as scientists call it, formulas. Numbers and symbols and letters comingling into their own language. I move on to the second page. The third. The fourth. Still mumbo jumbo. The fifth. Sixth. Seventh. *Guh.*

I'm beginning to think you have to be a genius to bring the dead back to life.

I keep searching and come across a section on gene splicing, but it has nothing to do with people. It focuses on the genes of peculiar creatures like the puffer fish, the mutable rainfrog, the wrap-around spider, and the mimic octopus. Where's the good stuff?

Continuing on, I find Experiment #1 in the middle of the book. In words I can understand. The experiments go all the way to #14 with hand-drawn illustrations sprinkled throughout. Each is chronicled with dates and time stamps from over *thirty* years ago. That's like two and a half of my lifetimes ago. Practically prehistoric.

Experiment #1 outlines the obvious. To reanimate someone, you need someone who needs reanimating. Someone dead. *Der*. It's right there in the title. How I glossed over that point until now is troubling since the thought alone of digging up a corpse gives me the willies, never mind actually doing it. And even if I did, then what? Drag it all the way home and lug it into the cellar with no one noticing? Unlikely. It's settled. No one's digging up anyone.

I'll stick to the replication aspect and cultivate my friend in a petri dish using my own DNA like a sane person. I know firsthand from when we did our 23andMe tests (thanks to Dad going overboard and wanting all the deets on our inner makings after Mom got ill) that a little bit of spit contains all your DNA, and I've got spit to spare. Enough for a dozen friends, easy.

I turn my attention to the crates of dangerous substances, speculating which contains the magic formula to sprout life. "Eeny, Meeny, Miney, Moe" lands on VOLATI E, and I'm not one to argue with this tried-and-true method of decision-making.

Even though the massive crate is solid wood, someone did

a half-fast job (as Dad assures me he's saying when it sounds like something else) of nailing it shut, and I'm able to muscle it open. I push the heavy piece of wood until it teeters on the edge, giving myself enough room to peruse the contents.

Empty.

To be sure, I scour the interior with my light, and get a glint of something. My flashlight does a double take as I swoop back to the something. A shiny silver metal tube, about the size of a cigar. This is an awfully big crate for one tiny item.

I hoist myself over the rim, bent at the waist, feet dangling, and reach for the tube at the bottom of the crate while trying not to fall in.

Gotcha.

I leap back to solid ground and size up my find. There's nothing written on the tube or the seal around the cap to identify it. It's light. Maybe it *is* a cigar.

Bracing myself, I shake it very gently. It is volatile, after all. It doesn't explode, but there's the faint clinking of an object hitting the inside of the metal tube. So, not a cigar.

I twist the cap.

The seal snaps and a hiss of air escapes. I squeeze my lips shut and hold my breath for ten Mississippis in case it's an ancient spirit looking for a host body. Safe, I shine my light to see what's inside the tube.

A glass vial filled with glowing green slime. Jolly Rancher green.

Delicately, I tip the metal tube so the vial can slide out into my palm. It's warm. The thick liquid glows. All sorts of scenarios come to mind. Alien blood. Truth serum. Coke's secret formula.

Careful to keep the vial upright so I don't spill it, I remove the stopper and sniff the candy-colored slime, anticipating green apple. Nope. More like day-old puke. I hold it at arm's length, away from my nostrils, and scrutinize the gooey fluid. It shimmers and rolls as if it's alive. Stoked, I grab a petri dish to begin my first experiment.

Imagining a slice of pepperoni pizza is all I need to get my juices flowing, and I spit into the dish. Slowly, very slowly so I only use a single drop, I tilt the vial over my saliva. As a tiny bead of the gooey fluid crests the edge of the vial and falls toward the petri dish, Dad calls my name, and I nearly have a heart attack. He's right behind me.

I spin around to begin my defense, no longer careful with my precious slime, and a glob shoots straight up out of the vial and swan dives into the back of my shoe! *Ack.*

"Monty!" Dad calls again. He's not behind me, and I realize I must be directly below the kitchen. Dad marches off, and I bet a million bucks he's heading for the stairs.

For my room.

CHAPTER 6

With the vial sealed, I put it in its metal tube, twist the cap shut, and toss it into the crate.

Zigzagging through the cellar, I find my way back to the grating, relieved it didn't fold itself up while I was gone. I climb into the secret passageway and run all the way to the rope ladder. Heart pounding, I scramble up so hastily that I miss one of the rungs and slip, burning my arm on the rope. But I don't let go. I find the rung and continue my ascent until I pull myself through the trapdoor, squeezing past Watson, who greets me with profuse licking.

Dad's footsteps are on the stairs to my room now.

I shove Watson aside. "Stop, Watson."

In total Dad fashion, he knocks and goes right for the knob without waiting for permission. Frantic, I slide the plank in place and sit on it—*nothing to see here*—as Dad enters.

"Dinner's ready."

"There's no point in knocking if you're just gonna walk in, Dad."

"You didn't answer when I called you. I was concerned."

A likely story would've been my retort if my foot didn't spontaneously combust. Or that's how it feels anyway. A stabbing, burning pain, like a red-hot poker jabbing into my heel, spreading down my arch, and setting my toes ablaze. Sweat shoots out of every pore and drenches me, and now I'm desperate for Dad to leave.

"Sorry," I say, sitting on my shoe, hoping to stop the fire. I bite my lip to distract from the pain and taste blood.

Dad turns to exit, then turns back. He's not looking at me, though. I follow his eyes to the broken soy container and sticky milk residue on the floor. "Honestly, Monty."

"It was an accident. What do you want me to do? Sit here and stare at the ceiling?"

"I want you to go out and make friends."

"I tried! And as usual, everyone laughed at me and called me names."

Dad sighs sympathetically. "Maybe, I'm simply suggesting, you save the cape for inside."

Wow.

"I just don't like to see you get hurt, Monty."

Speechless.

Knowing he won't get more from me, Dad heads for the door. He stops again, this time when he notices the picture of me and Kyle with Mom at the zoo. Me and Mom in our magician outfits. *Yeah, that's right. Mom wore a cape too. Remember her?* He turns back with a remorseful look on his face, but I stare at the floor, not wanting to hear his sentiment right now. For once, he picks up on my mood.

"Hurry up and come down." Soon as he closes the door behind him, I rip off my shoe and bury my head in my pillow with a scream.

Dad rushes back in. "What happened? Are you okay?"

I look up innocently. "Nothing. What?"

"Didn't you scream?"

"No. Hunh-unh."

He holds, as if he can crack me, but I'm unbreakable. Now that my shoe's off.

"Okay," he says and leaves.

I blow on my singed toes until they cool, then heave my smoking shoe under the bed. Along with it goes the Band-Aid that was protecting my popped blister, apparently, because it's not on my heel anymore. Nosy Watson wriggles under the bed to get a sniff, but I snap my fingers to stop him.

"Leave it, Watson." I slip into another pair of sneakers, and the hard canvas rubs against my raw blister, but I don't care. Nothing hurts compared to that volatile slime. "Let's get some yum-yums."

Watson scampers out, tail wagging, and runs ahead of me down the stairs.

# CHAPTER 7

Kyle flings open my door, scaring me out of a deep sleep.

With a groan, I pull the covers over my head and make him disappear.

"Time to get up," he says.

"Go away. I'm sleeping."

He yanks the covers off the entire bed, throwing them to the floor.

"Hey! I just washed those last month."

"First day at your new school, butt-wipe. Don't want to be late."

"Bite me."

Kyle grabs my arm, playfully coming in like a great white, his mouth wide open. I shriek with laughter (I can't help it, he looks goofy) as I struggle to pull free. Did I mention he's got a foot and change on me? With that, at least fifty pounds. I'm helpless, and his big fat mouth chomps down on my forearm.

"Ow. Okay, okay." I concede because human slobber is worse than basset slobber.

"Hurry up. Dad's waiting."

I throw my legs over the bed, sitting up, and gaze out the window, anticipating a miserable day. Only when I glance over my shoulder as Kyle's leaving do I realize he's wearing a skirt. From Fifi's Boutique, I'm guessing.

"You look ridiculous," I call after. "Shave your legs."

"Can't find the razor," he calls back from the stairs.

I slip into the closest pair of jeans on the floor, next to the remains of a PB&J I brought up here after Dad's fiasco of a dinner last night. Watson's in the far corner of the room like he's been trying to make his way to my leftovers without having to go near the bed.

"What's wrong with you?"

Before he can answer, something tickles my heel, and I spin around, thinking Kyle snuck back in with a feather duster or something to harass me. "I'm up."

But he's not here. Perplexed, I peer under the bed and spot the culprit. "That's not disgusting at all."

Some sort of fuzzy mold is growing from my abandoned sneaker under the bed. Splotchy orange and brown and black. And there's a fleshy morsel in the center of the wooly stuff, as if the blister scab from my Band-Aid started the whole thing, except I know better. That volatile slime is ruining my favorite Vans. I shove the shoe farther under the bed so Watson can't get to it. "Remind me to bleach that when I get home."

Watson's edging around the wall, still too intimidated to snare his prey. I toss the sandwich over. He swallows it without chewing, then skitters out of the room, Flintstones style. I should probably get a rug.

I put on yesterday's tee, grab my sneakers, pick my favorite board, snatch my helmet off the floor, throw my backpack over my shoulder, and head downstairs. I intentionally leave my cape behind. Not because Dad told me to. First days are hard enough, and I don't need another cape flushed down the toilet.

In the kitchen, Dad's trying to make up for dinner with pancakes. I forgive him.

"This is exciting," he says. "All three Hyde boys starting school on the same day."

Poor Dad if this is what passes for excitement.

Kyle loads his plate with pancakes, then flings one at me like a Frisbee.

I catch it before it hits my face. "Nice."

"You're welcome," he says, aiming the syrup nozzle at me.

"Dad," I scream before he squirts, but Kyle rights the bottle as Dad turns to see him handing it to me.

"Monty, why are you yelling?"

Kyle grins. I sigh. This is how it always goes.

"No reason." I smother my pancake in syrup, roll it into a tight tube, and shove it in my mouth until it's gone.

Kyle devours four almost as fast.

"Where's your bag with your school supplies?" Dad asks me.

I'm one step ahead of him. "By the door, so I don't forget it."

Mission accomplished. He smiles. "Great. If you're ready, let's go."

"Wait. What? What do you mean, let's go? You're not going with me."

"Do you even know where your school is, Monty?"

"I know how to use Waze. I'm not going with my father. All the kids will laugh at me."

"He's already got enough going against him," Kyle says.

"Thanks." *I think.*

Dad's still not sold. "But it's off campus, and you're so young."

"I'm almost thirteen."

"Exactly," he says, like that proves his point and not mine.

"You can't do this to me. It's hard enough always being the new kid."

My pleas work. Dad turns to Kyle for the final word, and Kyle, for all his faults, understands the severity of this dilemma—no one should ever show up at junior high with his father. "Thirteen is a man in most cultures," Kyle says.

"Fair enough." Dad holds his hand out to me. "Phone."

I relinquish my cell, and he punches the address into Waze.

"It says ten minutes, but give yourself twenty. You don't just have to get there, you have to navigate through campus and get to your classroom."

"I know how school works, Dad." I take my phone back.

"All right, then. I guess this is it. I'll see you both when I get home tonight." He looks from me to Kyle and back to me again as if it's the last time he'll ever lay eyes on us.

I bolt before he hugs me.

Glen Witch Junior High is six blocks east of the main gate to Crampus.

Couldn't be easier to get to. Like Dad said, ten minutes by foot. Five by board if you have fun along the way.

I expected something akin to a run-down haunted castle— it's called Glen *Witch*, after all—but it's the standard brick building like every other middle school in the country. And much bigger than I anticipated, taking up the equivalent of two city blocks. Half of that belonging to the track and sports fields. Obviously, Glen Witch isn't just for students whose parents work at the university. *Der*. Hundreds of kids from Clear Rock converge and file in. Everyone seems to know someone, but me. Standing alone, I feel like an outsider. I am an outsider.

Then something magical happens. On her board, the cute girl from the skate park stops near the steps to the main entrance and stands there, alone. Lost. Like me. She looks around and our eyes meet. The Fourth of July goes off in my head. I can't believe it. Smiling, she waves at me.

I start to wave back as she calls out, "Hey, Ripper. Thrash."

She's looking through me, like I don't exist. She doesn't even see me. *I'm standing right here.*

Luckily, my hand is one step ahead and pulling the fix-my-hair move—which isn't easy when you're wearing a helmet. I spin to see who she's looking at. Mr. Popular and another guy skate toward her.

" 'S'up, Ella," Mr. Popular says, also looking through me. I'm not sure if he's Ripper or Thrash.

Ripper, Thrash. Seriously. If you have to advertise.

The guys meet up with her—*Ella*—and they enter the school together. Lags run to make it in as the first bell rings, but not me. The dread in the pit of my stomach creates an invisible force field, preventing me from advancing. I about-face and tear out on my board, heading for home.

The guard at the main gate to Crampus recognizes me and lets me in, no questions asked. Either that, or he lets everyone in, no questions asked.

When I reach my block, I keep an eye out for Kyle. For all I know, he doesn't have class until this afternoon. I crab-walk around the side of the house, avoiding windows, and find the cellar doors leading to my secret lab. *Terrific.* Giant padlocked chains circle the handles. So much for checking on my first experiment (not that I assumed much would develop overnight, but still). Now what am I going to do until school's out?

After sitting in the bushes by the side of my house for half an hour, unsure if Kyle's at home or in class, I head for the skate park. He doesn't skate, so I'll be safe there if I make it past the university undetected.

Before I reach the walkway that branches around the Science building, I spot Dad coming toward me. I forgot to even consider him. He's deep in conversation with a nerdy suit-and-bow-tie man and doesn't see me. I pop my board and run up the steps to the Science building to hide. Once inside, I duck into the stairwell and press against the wall, away from the door.

"I appreciate you taking the time to show me around, Dean Smith," I hear Dad say as they enter the building. "But I remember the campus fairly well and I'm sure you have better things to do."

Crickets! They're heading this way. I race down as they open the door to the stairwell.

"On the contrary," the dean says. "Your return is of the utmost importance to me. I must say I was rather surprised, however. Most alumni leave and never look back."

I break out of the stairwell into the basement, and a chill envelops me immediately. Not just temperature, but the whole vibe. Everything's grey. Floors, walls, doors. Smoke filters through the hallway, and the flickering fluorescent lights overhead make it look *Slender Man* eerie down here. All the room numbers begin with *L*. Labs. That accounts for the chemical-y smells. The place seems abandoned, with heaps of boxes, crates, carriers, and other science junk, except I hear classes in progress.

There's no way I can make it to the stairs at the other end of the hall before Dad emerges, but I run for it anyway. A second later, the stairwell door opens behind me, and I dive into a stack of empty cardboard boxes.

"I'm flattered you remember me from my college days, Dean Smith," Dad says.

As they get closer, I have to talk myself down from jumping out and confessing. Remorse and cooperation equal less punishment, but I'm not caught yet. I keep an eye on them through a tear in the cardboard. The dean's expression, which seems permanent, looks like he's sucking on a Sour Patch Kids. His grey hair is parted down the middle and glued to his head with precision, clashing with his bushy black eyebrows, which he probably thinks are hidden behind his thick-rimmed glasses. They stick out like spider legs.

"Any protégé of Doctor Petrovic is worth remembering," he says to Dad.

"Thank you."

"It's not a compliment."

Dad stops. Right next to the boxes I'm hiding behind. "I don't understand," he says as if he's never been insulted before. Welcome to my world.

"Students have had complaints. I'm relying on you to inform me of any unethical goings-on."

"You want me to spy?"

"The science department is low on funds, Rober—Doctor Hyde. Illicit research akin to what that lunatic did decades ago could close us. We can't risk any incidents before our fundraiser."

"If he's a threat to the department, why is he still here?"

"He has tenure, you know."

A *WHAM* sends me stumbling, crushing boxes, but Dad doesn't notice me because he's startled too. A door to one of the labs was thrown open so hard, it slammed against the wall.

Dr. Petrovic is in the hallway, arm circling like a windmill as he yells into the room. "Get out! Get out! Quickly. Everybody out!"

Students flee.

Everyone's running this way, even Dr. Petrovic now.

"Dean Smith, duck!" he says and tackles the dean to the ground at exactly the same time an explosion rips through the classroom.

Blood and guts everywhere.

Gross. Gross! I'm covered in slimy . . . Wait a minute. It's not blood or guts. It's . . . tomato.

Dr. Petrovic jumps to his feet and saunters back to class as if nothing happened. The students follow. Just a normal day here on Crampus.

Dad, also drenched in tomato innards, helps the dean to his feet.

Dean Smith throws his hands in the air, exasperated. "Another prized tomato down the drain." He pivots and marches off, distraught.

Poor Dad. He stands there, motionless. All by himself. He actually looks the way I feel most of the time. Maybe that's a good thing. Maybe he'll take this as a sign, and we can hightail it out of here.

Nope. He's going into the classroom. *Whatever.*

I wipe the prized-tomato guts off me and escape this hall of horrors.

As planned, I go to the skate park. Aside from a few college kids, I've got the run to myself, and I spin fat kickflips, McTwists, and frontside flips.

How ya like me now? I'd totally say if Ella were here.

CHAPTER 8

My first experiment was a complete failure.

The saliva in the petri dish dried up without any signs of life. Instead of bumming out over it, I turn my secret lab into the ultimate hideout by adding posters, *TransWorld SKATEboarding* magazines, a beanbag chair, Oreo Double Stuf, Sprite, and a plastic cooler filled with ice. That way, I can practically live down here until I succeed in my quest.

I have three full hours before Dad gets home, and lots of ideas after deciphering parts of the journal. My hypothesis (that's science jargon for *guess*) is that I need to combine several serums to create the desired effect. Meaning, there must be more gooey stuff down here.

I break open the OXIC and POI ONOUS crates, and find a multitude of flasks buried deep in packing peanuts. Each contains a different liquid, ranging from thick and slimy to frothy and pulpy to clear as water. Thankfully, they all have stoppers that keep them from spilling.

Next, I retrieve the cigar tube with the vial of glowing green slime in it. I'm more confident now than ever that it's important because it hurt my foot too much to not be important. Plus, it grew that mold super fast inside my shoe, and mold is living organism.

Goggles on—safety first—I line up six test tubes in a rack and fill each one halfway with a different serum from the flasks, then put the flasks aside. I don't want to use everything up on one experiment. Aiming for the thickness of blood, I add a smidge from this tube and a tad from that one to a beaker on the Bunsen burner until I'm satisfied with the consistency. I top it all off with a drop of the infamous green slime.

While that's brewing, I rummage through unlabeled boxes for more supplies and discover a rabbit's foot. Hold everything. That counts as something that was once alive and is now dead. Talk about lucky. (Me, not the rabbit.) I have a corpse to reanimate. A real-life dead corpse. And I didn't even have to rob a grave.

I thrust my arm into the air, like Dr. Frankenstein would, and exclaim, "Experiment number two is afoot." I chuckle at my pun as I place the rabbit's foot on the lab table.

Using an eyedropper, I extract some of my concoction from the beaker on the Bunsen burner, then squeeze it onto the furry appendage.

I wait. And wait. And wait.

Nothing happens. Zero. Zilch. Not even a sizzle.

As I make a note of my second failed attempt in the back of the journal, I hear scratching on metal. I whip my eyes to the rabbit's foot. It's pulsating. For real. Little breaths, in and out. Its tiny nails scraping the table.

It's alive!

It didn't evolve into a whole rabbit or sprout eyes or ears, but it's definitely living. Undulating like a caterpillar, my fuzzy little friend inches toward me. It's so cute.

Or is it?

Suddenly, I'm not sure. Its fur stands on end, exposing its fang-filled mouth, and its claws grow razor sharp before my eyes.

I back away slowly.

In response, the mutant foot trembles and whimpers. On the edge of the table, it reaches out to me, crying.

My heart squeezes in sorrow. "Aw." I hurt its feelings. Looking at it now, I see nothing vicious about it.

I offer my hand, and it springs on me, in attack. I shriek and try to rip it off, but its claws dig into my arm, drawing blood. It squeals a horrifying, rabid squeal, burrowing in deeper, shredding my flesh. I can't get a good grip on it; it's too squirmy and strong. Unable to pull it off, I slam my arm into the wall. The foot screeches in pain, releasing its grasp, and drops to the floor with a squishy thud.

I scramble back, not taking my eyes off that fuzzy monster, and wrap my injuries with an old shirt from one of the clothing racks. The mutant's claws retract, and it whimpers again. A sad, soulful weep. It's heartbreaking. Maybe with love and obedience school it can be tamed.

Willing to give it a go, I search for a broom and dustpan so I can scoop it up without being in striking range, but when I return to the lab area, I'm too late. My specimen is dead.

I bow my head in a moment of silence, then sweep it up and drop it in the box I found it in. Some people might be discouraged, but this is a success in my book.

Snoring drills my eardrums like a jackhammer.

I toss and turn and kick the blankets off the bed, but none

of it lulls me to sleep. Patience depleted, I bolt upright. "Quit snoring, Watson."

Watson stares at me, wide-eyed, innocent. Tucked in a tight ball—the kind when he's nervous or scared or has been a bad boy—he whines. But he's definitely not snoring.

I put my ear to the floor to determine if it's Dad, and from the blackness under my bed, two bulbous eyes stare right at me.

"Agh." I somersault backwards, away from the bed, and tuck into my own tight ball next to Watson. Watson's all over me, pawing, licking, thrilled to have an ally. "Watson, stop, please." He calms, and I peek under the bed again.

"Oh, gross." Whatever it is has made itself at home in the wooly mold in my shoe. Which I obviously forgot to bleach.

A silent but deadly goes off, and I cover my nose. "Ew, Watson." He farts when he's nervous, but this one's for the record books. I slide him away from me and crouch lower on the floor to get a better look at the thing.

Its eyes are huge for its size, and it doesn't have a nose, exactly, more like two slits, which might account for the snoring. Its wrinkly skin is almost translucent. At first, I think it might be a baby mole or preemie raccoon that Watson brought up here—his penchant for gifting me geckos was a dark time in our past, darker for the geckos—but as I study it further, I realize it's not lying in the mold, it *is* the mold. Or rather, what I mistakenly thought was mold is actually the creature's orange and brown and black fur. Or hair. Or both. Whatever it is, it's a tangled mess.

My mind wends to the one plausible conclusion given all the facts: that green slime is the replication serum. Period.

It's the only thing that makes sense.

When that glob fell into my shoe, it must've mixed with my

blister pus or skin cells or nail fragments—or all of the above—and germinated into this life-form.

"Watson," I whisper in near disbelief. "I did it. I *made* a friend."

Watson silently farts again.

Using my magic wand, I gently nudge the shoe to see if the thing inside is as ferocious as the mutant rabbit's foot. The creature sucks in a breath and sighs adorably enough to hug, despite its disgusting larva-like appearance. It closes its eyes and snores.

Not knowing what else to do, I grab the blanket I kicked onto the floor and ball it up to create a comfortable place for my new friend. I'm not sure how long it will live, but it already outlasted the rabbit's foot. That's a good sign. Carefully, I slide the shoe out from under the bed and place it in the center of the balled-up blanket without waking (or touching) the creature.

Watson and I stare at it. After a moment, we look at each other, then back at the thing. We both giggle.

CHAPTER 9

Once again, my bedroom door flying open is my alarm clock.

This time, it's Dad. "Did you skip schoo—why are you on the floor?"

Groggy, I rub my eyes, trying to remember where I am. Oh, yeah. I fell asleep next to my new friend. My friend! I whip my gaze to the center of the blanket, but the creature is gone, shoe and all.

"Monty," Dad says. "Why are you on the floor?"

"I fell off the bed."

"With your blanket?"

"I guess," I say with a shrug as I get to my feet.

Dad grabs the blanket and shakes it. I flinch, expecting the creature to be ejected from within, but only dust particles fly off.

"Did you skip school yesterday?"

"Obviously." There's no point in lying. He knows.

"Get dressed. You've earned yourself an escort, young man." He places the blanket on my bed.

"I don't want to go."

"It's not up for negotiation. And before you protest, can you please try to see the positive side of this? School is a wonderful place to meet new kids."

"For who?"

"Oh, Monty." Dad cups my cheek in his hand, which has become his way of showing affection now that I skirt his hugs. "I know making friends isn't easy for you, but you have to give it a chance, okay?"

I push his hand away. "You don't get it."

"Then tell me."

"We're gonna move in six months like we always do. What's the point of trying to fit in?"

"It's not my intention to keep moving, and I know it's hard on you, but I'm doing the best I can. I really am."

"See? You don't get it."

Dad shakes his head in defeat. "Please get dressed and come down." He leaves.

I keep quiet until he reaches the bottom of the stairs, then tear through my room in search of the creature. What a nightmare. There's no sign of it anywhere, and Dad's bellowing for me already.

No choice, I spin to Watson. "You're on creature patrol. I'm counting on you to protect it and *not* rip the stuffing out of it. It's not a toy."

I throw on some clothes and hurry downstairs, eager to get school over with so I can return and look for my friend, but Watson charges past me in a beeline for the front door, reminding me he's got urgent business to take care of too. I give him three minutes on the front lawn to empty his bladder. Poop will have to wait.

I try not to let it bother me too much that Dad gets what he wanted all along.

To walk his almost-teenager to junior high. It would've been nice to know that an automated text goes out to parents when a kid doesn't show up. At least I could've prepared a preemptive excuse.

I give Dad the silent treatment the whole way, but when we reach the door to my classroom, I plead for mercy. "C'mon, Dad, don't go in with me. Everyone will laugh. Let me go in alone. I promise I won't skip school again."

"I want to speak to your teacher."

"What for?"

"To introduce myself."

"Why? Are you trying to ruin my life?"

"Monty, please stop making a big deal out of this."

Gaaaaaaaaaahhhhh. I fling open the door, and it hits the wall with a bang. Everyone turns and my face ignites.

"Sorry," Dad says with a sheepish smile. I can't tell if he's taking the blame or apologizing on behalf of his lunatic son. He talks quietly with the teacher—most likely telling her I'm weird or have a hard time making friends or something equally embarrassing—while I'm on display at the front of the room, looking down.

Kids whisper and laugh until the teacher claps her hands to get their attention. "Class, this is Montague Hyde. He's new to the neighborhood, so let's welcome him."

Unenthusiastic hellos bounce around, but I'm still counting specks on the tile floor. Only when the teacher says "Go on and take a seat, Montague" do I look up.

"Monty," I say.

Her expression doesn't change, and I take that to mean she'll be calling me Montague for the rest of the year. Scanning the rows, I find one available seat in the room, at the back of the class. Next to Mr. Popular.

Mr. Freaking-Popular.

As I head down the row, a guy sticks his foot out, tripping me. Yep. Same old, same old. I take my seat and Mr. Popular smirks.

"Where's your cape, daddy's boy?" he whispers.

I whisper right back. "Ooh, burn, I have a father."

He glares at me. "Dweeb."

"Jackass." I forget to whisper and everyone laughs. Everyone except Dad and the teacher.

"Montague Hyde, you apologize right now," Dad says, mortified.

Mr. Popular turns to me with a wide grin.

"Sorry," I say. Then mouth *jackass* when the grown-ups aren't looking. Watson isn't the only stubborn one in the family.

Mr. Popular threatens me with narrow eyes, and I shrug as if he doesn't scare me. He does, and I spend recess and lunch hiding in the library.

It's not until I'm rushing to fifth period that I see Ella. So far, we have no classes together, and it's not looking good for fifth either, because I'm heading to the room at the end of the hall and she's heading away from it. Toward me. Heart palpitations. Sweaty palms. Is there a red brighter than cherry? That's what my face is; I feel it. Still, I can't squander this opportunity to say hello. I wait to catch her eye, and at the exact moment she meets mine, two girls emerge from a classroom, screaming excitedly, "Magdiela!" They whisk her away, speaking Spanish.

I smile. *Note to self: sign up for Spanish Club.*

I don't cross paths again with Mr. Popular until last period—PE.

He's on the tennis team, and I'm not, so the only risky place is the locker room. Lucky for me, I don't have my gym clothes yet and I go straight to the gymnasium.

By the time school's out, I can barely riddle a heelflip off the steps. Dodging bullies is exhausting. Suddenly, I'm struck from behind so hard my breath is knocked out of me, and I'm sailing through the air. Feels like a Mack truck. I cushion the landing with my arms and roll to my feet. I'd totally get kudos for that if I were hit by a truck. But I wasn't.

Mr. Popular leans in. "You got something you wanna say to my face, poser?"

I grab my board and walk, but Mr. Popular yanks me back by the shirt.

"What's the matter? Chicken now that your daddy's not here to protect you?"

Kids start gathering, and I'm having PTSD flashbacks from all my other first days at a new school.

"Come on, daddy's boy," he taunts. "Put up or shut up."

Adrenaline kicks in. Fight or flight? I have a lot of practice outrunning bullies, but Ella shoves her way to the front of the crowd, and all I can think is I have a chance to be her new hero.

"Anytime, jackass," I say.

Bam. His fist hits my nose. The impact is like a thousand needles. My eyes water. Blood spurts everywhere. A synchronous "Oh!" from the crowd tells me it's bad. I ram him, grabbing him by the waist and tackling him to the ground. He pulls me with him, and fists are flying. I think some of them are mine.

A merry-go-round of yelling, goading, laughing faces blurs past, and I can't tell if Ella's is one of them. The world spins faster. My stomach aches. I want to vomit. But I keep swinging. And getting hit. Bells ring, and I think I'm late for class then remember school is out, and it's my head that's ringing.

The crowd goes wild with cheers, all of them for Ripper. So he's Ripper.

CHAPTER 10

My eye is so swollen, I can see it.

Dad sits next to me outside the principal's office. "What were you thinking?"

"He started it."

"Did he? Are you sure you didn't provoke him with some name-calling?"

"Yeah I'm sure! And for your information, he called me a name first."

"Ease up on the tone, Monty."

Ugh. It's always my fault.

The door opens, and Ripper exits the principal's office. I got a few good punches in, because his left cheek is blue and his lip is split. He doesn't meet my gaze, and I consider that a win. Dr. Petrovic exits after him, scratching his wooly hair as if the idea of a fight perplexes him. He looks at Dad with his good eye while his wonky eye sizes me up. Dad gives the doctor a sympathetic shrug, but before words can be exchanged, the principal calls us in. With a terse smile, she motions to two chairs opposite her immaculately organized desk.

I sit in silence as Dad does the heavy lifting, making promises I don't know I can keep. But it's nice to hear him sing my praises. I'm a good kid. Top of my class. Team player. Never been in a fight before. (That he knows of.) Won't happen again.

Apparently, the school has a zero-tolerance policy for aggressive behavior. Except when it's perpetrated by the grandson of "the esteemed, revered, he's done so much for the community" Dr. Petrovic. That's right. The guy who hates my guts is the grandson of my dad's boss, and as such, can bully the new guy without consequence, evidently.

His preferential treatment spills onto me, and I get off with a warning. And a lecture.

"I understand it's difficult to leave friends behind and go to a new school," the principal begins, "but life is full of challenges, son. The key is to face them with integrity and honor. Here at Glen Witch, we pride ourselves in shaping the morality of our graduates. Think of us as family."

Barf. "Can I go now please?"

"Monty," Dad says.

"What? I said please."

"We demand our students respect one another, Montague. That means you put aside your differences and get along. Understood?"

"Yes."

"You may go," the principal says.

I'm out the door, but I hear Dad say, "He really is a good kid."

"A delight, I'm sure," she replies.

Wretched day. First, Dad walked me to school, now he's walking me home. "Fighting is no way to make friends, Monty."

"So I'm supposed to stand there and take it?"

"Well . . . no . . ."

"Then what?"

It's not often I stump Dad, but he's got no answer.

"Straight home after school the rest of the week."

"You mean I won't get to hang out with all my friends?"

"Fair point. No skateboard the rest of the week," he amends.

What? Wait. "Why? I only defended myself."

"Because fighting is bad. You should've walked away."

"I tried."

"Did you? Honestly?"

Aaaaaaagggggghhhhh. I can't tell him I wanted to impress a girl. "Fine." It's not like my life doesn't suck already anyway.

Desperate for good news, I take the stairs three at a time all the way to the attic.

Only Watson greets me. With a yawn, no less. Disappointed my fuzzy little friend didn't return, I pace to think up my next move, and immediately trip over the trapdoor. It's dislodged slightly.

"Watson, look. Our first clue." The creature must've fled down there to hide when it heard Dad coming up the stairs to my room.

I push the trapdoor open and slide in, taking the rope ladder to the secret passageway. FYI, total darkness is scary, especially when an unknown life-form could be traipsing about.

"Hello?" I whisper. "Are you here?"

Silence.

I forge ahead. The grate to the cellar remains unfolded, and I gently descend. I'm relieved the bulb hanging over the lab tables is still on and hasn't burned out. "Hello?"

Nothing.

"Hello," I say with authority this time, but still get no response.

I continue toward the lab area and find an empty package of Oreos and two crushed cans of Sprite by the cooler. I'm thrilled and nervous in equal parts; the creature is definitely here. I pick up the cans to throw them away and notice the tabs are unopened, and there are two puncture holes in each can. Like fangs. Before I can fully process that bit of information, a clump of orange and brown and black fur shoots out from under the metal table, and I leap back with a scream. It vanishes into the shadows.

Once I stop hyperventilating, I warble, "Don't be scared. I won't hurt you."

Apparently, my quavering voice doesn't convince the creature I'm not a threat, and it remains in hiding. But the empty Oreos package gives me an idea. I'll lure it out.

I sprint back to the secret passageway, up to my room, down to the kitchen to collect bait, out to the garage to get supplies, including Watson's crate, then back up to my room without taking a moment to rest.

Using rope, I lower Watson's crate into the passageway. Suddenly, it means the world to him, and he pouts, head hanging over the trapdoor opening like he's watching his best friend being buried. I'll console him later. I hop in and take the ladder down like a pro.

The crate is almost as wide as the passageway, but I'm able to grab hold of the top, wrapping my fingers through the metal wire, to carry it through. It bangs against my shins the entire way, making me long for my pads as a buffer, but I don't stop running.

In my hideout, I place it near the beanbag chair as though it's a piece of furniture. *Nothing out of the ordinary here.*

Sacrificing another pack of Oreos and a can of Sprite, I rig the opened door of the crate to drop shut once the food inside is touched. Pleased, I take a moment to admire my genius, then head back up to my room to wait.

Prostrate on the floor with my ear to the trapdoor, I listen for progress. At some point, I doze off until Watson kicks me in his sleep with one of his squirrel-chasing dreams. It's almost 2 a.m., but I'm wide-awake like Christmas morning. I race down to the cellar to see if my plan worked.

The door to the crate is closed and the food is gone, but there's no creature inside. The crate is empty. Bummed, I kick the beanbag chair and the fuzzy thing darts out from behind it.

"Agh!"

It is way bigger and furrier than before, almost Watson-size, and it's wearing my Vans sneaker! It zips up the stairs to the cellar doors above the crates and, like a cartoon, impossibly squeezes through the small gap in the doors.

Holy frijoles! It left the house!

"Wait. Come back." I bound up the steps to the cellar doors, but only my arm can fit through the gap. "Come back," I shout through the opening as I shake the doors, trying to break the chains.

"No, no, no." This is bad.

I sprint full speed all the way back to my room so I can go out the conventional way—through the front door. It's pitch black outside, except for distant streetlamps casting dim cones of light, and the creature is nowhere in sight.

I take off running, weaving in and out of every block in the neighborhood, scouring every nook and cranny, climbing trees and shaking bushes, checking unlocked cars and trespassing into backyards, peeping through windows and crawling into dog houses, ripping open mailboxes and digging up flowerbeds, until my body is rubber. Against my will, I fall to the ground, too weak, physically and emotionally, to move.

The failure gives me a stomachache. I'm the one who scared it out of the house, and now it's wandering around all alone. Will it know how to survive in the wilds of Crampus?

When my pulse normalizes and I can breathe without gasping, I push myself up and head home. Fighting back tears, I sit on my porch steps. I can't bring myself to go in and give Watson the bad news.

CHAPTER 11

I manage a whole day at school without getting bullied.

(I don't count the eighth-grader who slammed my locker shut while I was putting my books away since he did that to everyone he passed.)

Nearly home, I hear wheels on cement behind me. Used to be my favorite sound. Now it gives me the terrors. I don't look back until I'm running up the steps to my house. It's Ella, not Ripper.

Ella.

We lock eyes. At least I think we do. Maybe she's looking right through me again.

"Stop gawking, dweeb."

Omigod, she *was* looking at me. I hurry in so she doesn't see my grin. Watson scrambles to greet me, but I leap over him and rush to the living room window to watch where she's going. *No way.* We're next-door neighbors if you don't count the two houses between us.

"Who you spying on, butt-wipe?"

"No one." I slam the curtains shut, yanking the rod off the wall.

Kyle peers over my head, but I'm safe. Ella's inside. He balances the curtain rod back on its bracket. "Dad's gotta work tonight, and Diego's having a party."

"So?"

"So do you have a friend yet, so you can sleep over at their place?"

"Why do I need to sleep at someone else's? I got my own bed upstairs."

"Because Dad's working late and I have a party to go to."

"I heard you the first time."

"You're saying you're not going to be afraid? All alone. In this big house. By yourself. No one else. Just. You."

Well, if you're gonna put it that way . . . But I find my courage. It's right next to my stubbornness. "Nice try."

"Cool." He stirs my hair into a nest, and I try to fight him off. "You'll be remembered fondly. Not by me, but by someone, I'm sure." He bolts up the stairs, leaving me swatting air. "I'll heat your dinner before I leave."

"Don't bother. I'm not gonna eat it." It's meatloaf. I saw the Tupperware with my name on it this morning. I grab the Lay's Family Size bag of barbecue potato chips and a Sprite. Much as I'd like to hit the lab, I know Kyle will check in on me before he leaves (not soon enough), and the last thing I need is for that bigmouth to find out about my secret hideout. He used to have my back, but ever since Mom died, he's been Team Dad.

I search for the perfect vantage point in the living room to monitor Ella's house: far enough away from the window so it doesn't look like I'm staring out creepily but close enough to see if she leaves. If she does, I'll leisurely exit so we can bump into each other.

As I pace, waiting for the stars to align, Watson trails me like a Roomba picking up crumbs. Sometimes I drop them on purpose. I polish off the bag of chips, finish the backwash of Sprite, and burp. Wet, long, and plangent.

"Epic," Kyle calls down from his room, and lets out a doozy of his own. I laugh. Maybe not everything has changed.

Fed up with fruitless spying, I grab my board and go out front to do some tricks. Watson watches from the porch. If I'm lucky, Ella will see I'm not a poser now that Ripper's not here to sabotage me. After five minutes of practicing ways to say hello in my head, I'm grateful she doesn't emerge. It doesn't even sound like a word anymore.

I'm doubly grateful for her absence when my nemesis rounds the corner across the street and ollies over to my side, skating toward me. Pretending I don't see him, I stroll back toward my house, prepared to casually flee for my life.

"Hey," he says, stopping on the sidewalk in front of my walkway as I meander up the porch steps, this-close to safety. His perfect face is healed whereas mine still sports green and yellow bruises. "Thrash is having a birthday party at D'Onofrio's. Wanna go?"

Do I? D'Onofrio's is the pizzeria by Glen Witch where all the kids hang out after school. I guess Ripper got the same lecture I did from the principal. "Sure," I say, my eyes as wide as my smile.

"Too bad. It's invitation only." He cracks up and moves on. *Jerk.*

I pivot to go inside, but Ella runs out of her house to meet up with him, and my mouth drops open in awe. Her long hair is flowing freely, not in a ponytail the way she usually has it. And she's wearing a white lacy top and flower-print shorts, not her baggy skater gear. Not that she doesn't look totally rad in skater gear, but this is a side of her I've never seen. It's like, you think Oreos can't get any better, and then Double Stuf. That's what she is right now. Double Stuf. I watch the whole way as the person I like the most exits the gates of Crampus with the person I hate the most.

Ow.

CHAPTER 12

Finally.

Kyle's at the party, and I have all night to purposely create what I accidentally created once before. A friend.

Not that I've given up on reuniting with my first creation. Lots of animals get loose and return home, often years later. But I have to be realistic too. It's possible it found a new home, a new friend, a new life. (Or the other thing I refuse to entertain at this point—the *D* word.)

For my current attempt, I've got Watson's giant hedgehog laid out on the metal table like a corpse. It's already coming apart at the seams and missing half its insides, making my job easier. I fill it with the only guts I could find in the kitchen: liver, ground sausage, and three eggs. Next, I duplicate the environment from inside my Vans where my first friend grew by combining a used Band-Aid with some new pus from my popped blister, a toenail clipping replete with toe jam, and some skin cells in the form of a cuticle I removed from my thumb, and I put that blend inside the plushy. Lastly, I add the same formula mixture I used on the rabbit's foot but increase the green slime to two drops, hoping that will make it live longer. I seal the stomach with duct tape.

I wait. And wait. And wait and wait and wait and *WHAM!* A door slams. Inside the house!

Somewhere.

Upstairs? Down here? I can't tell.

All I know is I dropped, tucked, and rolled under the table where I remain, trembling. Several minutes pass without any further noise. No footsteps. No scuffling. No screaming. No Watson barking crazily.

Stupid Kyle. Got into my head. It was probably a neighbor or a car backfiring or my imagination. It's definitely not an ax-wielding murderer.

Laughing it off, I crawl out from under the table and get back to work. I balance over the edge of the OXIC crate with my torso submerged in foam peanuts and dig for hidden ingredients.

CRASH. SMASH.

Okay, that was not my imagination. I snap my head around, and—"Aggghhh!"—the overstuffed hedgehog is in my face, snarling viciously.

Stunned, I fall into the crate, sending a plume of peanuts in the air. The rabid plushy swan dives off the lip, right for me, slimy liver and runny yolk seeping from its taped stomach.

"Aggggggggh!" When did it grow fangs?

In a dreamlike haze of panic, I start hallucinating and see a monstrous hairy hand snatch the hedgehog midair and pop it like a zit. But actual guts splatter everywhere—all over the foam peanuts, all over me—and I realize I'm not hallucinating.

Through squinched eyes, I glimpse a massive mouth, high above me, of ginormous jagged teeth that make *Jaws* look like a guppy. I leap out of the crate before it chomps down, and hightail it to the grate. There's a ruckus behind me—is it giving chase, is it destroying my lab?—but I never look back. I scale the grate faster than humanly possible, sprint through the passageway, fly up the rope ladder, and slide the trapdoor in place. I push my magic stand over the trapdoor to keep it secure, and race out of my room.

My brain is on turbo. The patchy fur. Orange, brown, black. The wrinkly flesh. Smelly, vile, repugnant. It's the thing, the creature, the *friend* I made—now supersized into a ferocious beast. I know I begged for it to return, but not like this. No one wants a rampaging monster.

I bolt out of the house, slamming the door before poor Watson can follow (*I'm sorry, buddy*), and run over to Diego's across the street. Music thumps loudly, and partiers scream louder than that. Wiping guts off of me, I push through the crowd looking for Kyle. There must be hundreds of people. On the front lawn, inside the house, in the backyard.

"Kyle! Kyle!" I yell at the top of my lungs and can't hear myself over the din of music and college kids. Lost in the sea of bodies, I get knocked around until I go down. I stay there, on my hands and knees, and scan the backyard. More guys than girls are wearing skirts. Pledges. A pair of unshaven legs in a silky skirt at two o'clock gets my attention. I crawl toward them then jump to my feet, rambling. "Kyle, I made a monster out of the science stuff in the—"

A girl stares back at me.

"You're not Kyle."

Hands grab me around the ribs from behind and hoist me up. It's the monster. My life is over. I kick and punch and scream until Kyle shouts in my ear, "Cut it out, Monty."

I go limp with relief, and he drops me to the ground.

"Kyle, I made a monster. I didn't mean to, but I did. It's in the house. You gotta come home."

Kyle drags me by the wrist to Diego's front lawn where we can talk without screaming. "Monty, I told you to sleep at a friend's. I knew you'd be scared."

"I'm not scared. Well, I mean, I wasn't, until I saw the monster."

"There's no such thing as monsters," Kyle says.

"That's what I thought, but there is. I made it."

"You made a monster? You can't even make your bed, but you made a monster?"

"Yes. I was trying to make a friend but—"

"Boo!" Diego says, sneaking up behind me, and of course, I jump. Everyone in earshot laughs, including Kyle. Diego hands him a beer.

"You guys suck!" I say, marching off.

"Watch your language, butt-wipe," Kyle calls after.

I barely make it to the street when I see, for sure, without a doubt, 100 percent, the curtains in my bedroom window rustle.

The monster. It's in my room. Watching me.

Run!

CHAPTER 13

My arms and legs go a million miles an hour.

A full moon hangs low in the sky, shredded by ragged clouds, and faint howls drift in the wind. My gut tells me I'm being chased, but I don't look back. Every time someone looks back in the movies, they trip and it's *adios*, thanks for playing. *Note to self: seriously, Spanish Club.*

Across campus, all the buildings are dark except the Science building. I beeline for the stairs to the entrance, take them three at a time, yank open the door, pull it shut, and finally look out as I hold the door closed with both hands and one leg. I don't see the monster, but it's shadowy outside. The movement could be branches, could be an ugly vicious life-form. I can't tell if I'm safe or vulnerable.

The light above me crackles. Over my shoulder, the hallway fades into darkness. I envision the monster slamming up against the glass doors and scare myself into letting go and running into the stairwell.

I fly down the stairs, rip open the door, and charge into the basement corridor. Smoke still wafts about eerily. The flickering fluorescent bulbs flicker no more down here, and I'm standing in a black void, except for a sliver of light at the end of the hall. The last door on the right is ajar just enough to allow optimism to surface. *Dad?*

I speed walk, trying to calm myself for the upcoming confession. He won't be happy I didn't tell him about the secret lab in our cellar, but I think I can get him to appreciate my accomplishment. He longs for me to take an interest in science, and it doesn't get more science-y than creating a living, breathing monster. Story straight in my head, I'm about to enter, but stop.

It's not Dad inside the lab, it's Ashanta. And she, a supposed doctor, kisses an industrial-sized refrigerator. "Good night, sweetie. I love you," she says. To the refrigerator.

She doesn't see me, which is good because I don't know what I'd say. The stairwell door behind me starts to open, and I snap to, remembering the monster. I take off around the next corner and zero in on a light coming from another one of the labs.

"Dad," I yell, running into the room and right into Dad, knocking whatever's in his hands up in the air.

"Noooooooo," Dr. Petrovic yells in anguish. He's also in the room.

Instinctively, I'm already reaching out, and I catch it before it hits the ground, then see, and feel, what it is. A heart. A real-life, firm but fleshy, disgusting organ. "Gross!"

I hot-potato it to Dad, and he catches it. He's wearing protective goggles and canvas gloves.

"Monty, what're you doing here? Are you okay?" He puts the heart in a square metal container about the size of those ice-cream freezers in 7-Elevens, except there's no glass to see inside this one, but I have a good idea based on the label.

CryogenOrgans. Next to the freezer, a metal cylinder as tall as me reads *Liquid Nitrogen*.

Cryogenics. I'm familiar.

On a metal table is a cadaver. At least I presume it is. It's covered entirely, except for a toe that sticks out one end.

"Monty," Dad says again, his face in mine, goggles up, brow furrowed with concern. "Why are you here? Did something happen?"

"I tried to make a friend, but I made a monster instead. I didn't mean to, Dad. I swear. It was an accident."

Like magic, the wild-eyed Dr. Petrovic appears next to Dad so now I've got two faces in mine. "Go on, dear boy, do go on," he says. He still smells like pastrami.

Dad takes my hand, leading me away so we have privacy. "Son, if you're afraid to stay home alone, it's nothing to be ashamed of."

"I'm not afraid," I say, pulling away. "There's a monster."

He gives me that look I hate—the one where he feels sorry for me. "I know I said I wouldn't work so much when we moved this time, but I promise things will let up soon. And then I'll be home every night." He tries to hug me but, I push him away.

"Stop it, Dad. I've been alone enough times to not be afraid to be alone. I'm telling you, there's a monster in the house."

"Okay. Okay. What's this monster's name?"

I stare, too dumbfounded to speak. You have one imaginary friend when you're six years old, and now everything must be make-believe. "Godzilla," I say.

"Godzilla, huh?"

Seriously. I march out.

"Monty," he calls from the doorway.

"I'm going home. Is that okay?" I round the corner, but two steps into the dark hallway, I remember my predicament and stop to listen for raging monsters. All I hear is Dad in the lab.

"Ever since . . . well, he and his mother were so close. She used to teach him magic tricks. More fun than science," Dad says with a wistful laugh. Then he sighs. "Poor Monty. He really thought magic could save her."

My lip trembles, betraying my will. Too outraged to be scared, I march down the hall, up the stairs, bypass a security guard—who demands to know what I'm doing here as he's about to lock up—fling open the doors to the outside, and keep going.

Bob's Arcade is jammed.

That's the gaming place around the corner from Glen Witch where teens ditching school and college kids hang out during the day. Right now, there's more of a rowdy crowd, but it beats going home to a monster.

Broke, I wander through, pretending I'm looking for a machine and not merely killing time. Two guys, older than Kyle—maybe in their twenties—watch me. One of them has tattoos pretty much everywhere I see skin, and the other one has a buzz cut with a *Z* shaved on the side. I act like I don't notice them staring me down, and pick up my pace as if I found the game I was looking for.

Buzz Cut motions to me with his head. "Where you from?"

I keep walking. It's loud in here. Plausible I didn't hear him.

He grabs my arm. "I said where you from?"

"I heard you."

His friend laughs.

"I didn't hear your answer," he says.

"Nowhere," I say, then turn to his friend who has a pack of

Marlboros in his pocket. "You got an extra cigarette, man?"

Both guys laugh now. "You smoke?" the smoker says.

"Only when I'm stressed." He doesn't give me a cigarette, which is good. I'm short enough already.

"Why you out by yourself this late?" Buzz Cut says.

I shrug. "Because I can be."

He grins like I said something useful to him. "What's your name, kid?"

"Monty."

"That's Elmo. I'm Zippy," Buzz Cut says, and I kind of don't believe him despite the capital *Z* on his head. "I ain't seen you before. You just move here or something?"

"Yeah." *Why?*

"You go to Glen Witch?" Elmo asks.

"Sometimes."

"Sometimes," Elmo repeats like I'm a riot. I relax and laugh a little. These guys aren't so bad. "Still want that smoke?"

"Nah, I'm trying to quit."

"Smart," Elmo says, tossing a cigarette up and catching it in his mouth.

Zippy pats me on the shoulder. "You need anything, let me know and I'll hook you up."

"Sure."

People make way as Zippy and Elmo head for the exit. Funny, the scariest guys I meet are the nicest ones to me since I moved here.

Hours past my bedtime, I stagger home exhausted.

On my block, two police cars with flashing lights are parked at an angle, barricading the street in both directions. Inside their barricade, right in front of Diego's house, is a paramedic truck. Students huddle and cling to each other, looking aghast. My stomach dives in despair, assuming the worst, and I slow my gait, afraid to approach. *Kyle?*

Kyle emerges from the crowd, and I weaken with relief, nearly buckling. He, however, storms over like he's going to shove me to the ground. I brace for impact, but he pulls me in for a hug.

Then he shoves me back.

"Damn it, Monty, where were you? I texted a million times."

"Out. Nowhere. What's going on?"

"Sam and Beth were attacked by some maniac. I came home to check on you, and you were gone, you butt-wipe."

"Attacked? You mean killed?"

"Beth got away but . . ." Kyle swallows, having difficulty continuing. "No one can find Sam. It happened so fast. Beth said all she could remember were hairy arms clawing at them."

I choke on my own gasp. Hairy arms. Claws. The monster. My throat turns to sandpaper, and I can barely speak. "Monster."

"You got that right. Anyone who'd do something like this is a monster."

"No. I mean, it *is* a monster. A real one."

"Stop with your stupid prank, Monty. A person might be dead. Have some respect."

"I'm telling you, Kyle, there's a monster. I created it. I didn't mean to, but—" The realization punches me in the stomach, taking my breath. *I* created it.

This is my fault.

CHAPTER 14

The magic stand remains over the trapdoor, undisturbed.

That means the monster must've left through the cellar to go on its spree. That, and the fact that Watson's still in one piece. Much as I wish it would move on to another town and be someone else's problem, it's my responsibility to take care of this. Besides, I'm certain it thinks my hideout is its home. If it's not back already, it will be after it's found someone else to eat.

I drop to my hands and knees, and put my ear to the floor to make sure it's not exploring its way up here. So far, so good. I know it's not in the main part of the house because Kyle locked all the doors and windows and we checked all the closets when we came in. Me because of the monster; Kyle because he thinks there's a maniac on the loose. Same diff.

Keeping a baseball bat next to me for protection, I divide my attention between watching the magic stand for signs of movement and doodling various ideas to capture my creation. Without a cannon or bear trap at my disposal, a lasso seems to be my best bet.

I stack boxes ten feet high as a stand-in for the monster and start practicing. A floor lamp is my first victim. Then I yank a blade off the ceiling fan, and snag the bedpost, but eventually, I manage to land the lasso over the boxes. When I get three out of five, I consider the odds in my favor. Ideally, I can rope the monster like a cowboy ropes steer. No one has to get hurt.

Watson's not the type to abandon me, but I open my bedroom door in case things go bad. I want him to have an escape.

Having only two hands to speak of, there's no way I can effectively carry and use the baseball bat and the lasso and a flashlight, *and* climb down the ladder and the grate. The bat stays.

With the rope over my shoulder and the flashlight in my pocket for now, I slide the magic stand off the trapdoor and descend into the secret passage. The silence is more deafening than any action movie I've been to, and I'm left to imagine the monster lying in wait, ready to ambush me around every corner.

Flashlight off so as not to give myself away, I tread as silently as I can through the narrow confines. By the time I reach the cellar, my heart pounds hard enough to give me a headache. It's dark. Either the bulb burned out or the monster turned it off. I don't hear anything, though.

This place is too cavernous to traverse blindly so I have to turn on the flashlight. I sweep the beam from side to side as I ease my way through the junk. As I get closer to the lab, the blue flame of the Bunsen burner stands out in the darkness, and I race over, remembering that I fled mid-experiment. The beaker and its contents are charred black. I turn off the gas valve, thankful I didn't burn down the house.

I peek into the crate where I had my encounter—with both the hedgehog and the monster—and find it clean of splatter. No guts. Nothing but packing peanuts. A flicker of doubt shoots through my mind, but I fight it off. I don't care how many noxious fumes I breathed in down here, what I saw was real. The monster probably licked up the proof.

The cellar doors overhead rattle, giving me a start, and I launch my rope, whipping the charred beaker off table with the noose. The doors rattle again, mocking me. It's just the wind. No monster.

I slog back to the secret passageway, slouched in discontent.

Watson greets me with kisses when I return to my room, and to be honest, it makes me feel a little better.

I position the magic stand over the trapdoor again. That way, I'll hear the monster before it gets in if it comes up this way. Planning an all-nighter, I prop myself up in bed, gripping my baseball bat. I've also got my lasso beside me (determined to be calmer next time I unleash it).

By four in the morning, my head weighs a ton.

Next thing I know, my door flings open, and I jolt up, alarmed, swinging the bat to save my life. Kyle hits the floor, escaping my attack. The clock reads 8:14. It takes a moment to register that it's morning.

"Rise and shine, slugger." He slithers out but has the decency not to ask questions.

I scan my room. It's monster-free. Magic stand is where I left it.

The rest of the weekend goes without incident. No monster sightings (or attacks) inside or outside the house. No police barricades or paramedics in the neighborhood. And best of all, I glimpse Ella from my living room window as she passes by on her board. Twice.

CHAPTER 15

Monty, let's go," Dad calls from the second floor.

Yeah, he's still walking me to school. But after another night spent on monster patrol, gripping the baseball bat, I'm nauseous with tiredness. I don't have to fake a sick voice. "I don't feel good."

"All right. I'll take you to the doctor."

Aggghhh. "Never mind!"

My fingers ache as I unpeel each one from the bat. I wiggle them to get my circulation going. Sitting on the bed so I can put my jeans on two legs at a time, I barely get my feet in when something fuzzy pushes into my shoulder blades. I bolt. And face-plant into the wood floor, thanks to the pants around my ankles. Weaponless, I flip onto my back to confront the monster, hands swatting the air.

On my bed, Watson stares at me with one of his stuffed toys in his mouth. "Watson, darn it!" I don't know if I'm miffed or relieved. But we tug-o'-war it a few times—he's easy to please—then I leave the horror of home and head to the horror of school.

Ripper's not in first period, and maybe it's my imagination

but the air is fresher, the room brighter, the mood cheerier. At recess, I splurge and buy two granola bars from the vending machine. Ella likes the Chewy Chocolate Chip ones. She's the first to show up at their usual table in the quad, and Thrash arrives a second later. I watch from my locker, which is outside, on the side of the building next to the quad. Apparently, outdoor lockers are a thing when you live somewhere where it doesn't snow.

I'm determined to approach the table. Thrash doesn't hate me as much as Ripper does; we have Social Studies together, and he basically ignores me. I close my locker, and both granola bars are snatched from my hand.

Ripper.

He doesn't say anything; he keeps going until he reaches Ella and gives her one of the bars. He eats the other.

I'm disappointed in myself for thinking I got off easy. But I don't dwell too much because my favorite part of the day is ahead of me. Fifth period. That's when Ella and I pass each other in the halls. Maybe I can ask her about the Spanish Club. Is she even in the Spanish Club? Why am I assuming she's in the Spanish Club just because she speaks Spanish? Why am I saying Spanish so much? Maybe I'm overthinking this whole thing. Am I overthinking? Obviously, if I have to ask, I'm overthinking.

I take a different route to fifth period.

School out for the day, I sail off the steps on my board.

Ripper, Thrash, and some other guy (whose name I don't know) skate toward me threateningly. I wonder how Ripper got out before me. Ever since I found out we both have PE for last period, I always wear my gym clothes under my regular clothes to avoid the locker room and get a head start home. He must've skipped tennis for the occasion. I pull a 180, but Thrash and the other guy haul butt and cut me off, making me abandon my board.

"Dude can't even roll," Ripper says with a smirk.

Ignoring him, I head for my board, but he grinds to a halt in my face, impeding me from continuing.

The crowd oohs. Yeah, there's a crowd. And naturally, Ella's making her way in to witness my impending doom.

"Oh, am I in your way?" Ripper says.

I take a step to go around him, but he kickturns in front of me so that he's blocking my path. I go the other way and he does too.

"What's the matter?" he says. "Can't get around?"

From somewhere in the mix of snickering onlookers, I hear, "You doggin' my boy, punk?"

It's Zippy. Of Zippy and Elmo. Both of them emerge, and Ripper's swagger shrinks.

"Nah, we were just talking, right, Monty?" Ripper says.

The picked-on part of me wants to rat him out and see what happens, but Ella. "Yeah, talking."

Zippy towers over Ripper. "Better not hear otherwise."

Ripper does the smart thing and nods to his friends. "Let's split."

They skate off, Ella included, but she gives me a sideways glance, and I don't know what it means. Is she impressed? Incensed? Do I have broccoli in my teeth?

Zippy and Elmo laugh and I join in, but I really want to skate off with Ella.

CHAPTER 16

Fog cloaks my house.

Only mine.

Other than Kyle's bedroom light on the second floor, it's dark inside, which means I lucked out because Dad's working late again. Zippy and Elmo insisted on treating me to some games and pizza at the arcade, and after saving my butt, it seemed rude to refuse. Plus, they're really nice to me.

The door creaks as I sneak in, and Watson emerges from the shadows, his long nails clacking on the wood floor.

"Shhhh."

I tiptoe toward the stairs, and the hallway lights on the second floor go on. Kyle glares at me from the top of the stairs. Still in his pledge skirt.

"Look, Watson, it's Mom."

Kyle doesn't crack. "Where've you been? You're supposed to come straight home from school."

"Loosen your girdle," I say, passing him on my way to the third floor. "It's pinching in all the wrong places."

"I asked you a question, butt-wipe."

"I don't give a fig. You're not my keeper."

"Hey!" he calls after, but I march down the hall without looking back.

I'm about to jog up the stairs to the attic and stop. My door is ajar, and I'm sure I closed it when I left this morning. I take the squeaky stairs as lightly as I can and gently push the door. My body stiffens instantly.

The magic stand. It's open. Top hinged up.

Kyle appears next to me, and I jump with a yelp. I didn't even hear him coming.

"This isn't a joke, Monty. Another student disappeared. There's a maniac on the loose."

I know! It's the monster!

"Pull this crap again and I'm telling Dad," Kyle continues, and I realize I didn't speak out loud.

"The monster," I whisper because I can't find my voice, like in those nightmares when you're trying to scream for help but your throat is paralyzed. "It's in here somewhere."

Kyle pushes me into the room. "Lame."

After a stumble, I catch myself and freeze, hearing nothing but Kyle's footsteps descending the stairs. I don't want to, but I know I have to secure the room. Speckled with goosebumps of fear, I crouch down and check under the bed. Only the usual dust bunnies. Grabbing my handy bat, I turn to the closet next and rip open the door. "Yah!" I don't know why I say that, it just comes out. But there's no monster in the closet, anyway.

The trapdoor on the floor is still in place, and the magic stand is empty, other than my props. Time for Plan B.

I fill a plastic bucket from the kitchen with ice water, grab a small table lamp from the living room, and steal the line from Dad's fishing pole (that he used once but keeps for sentimental reasons).

Back in my room, I rig it all together. I tie the fishing line from the window, across the magic stand, setting it to trip the lamp (I've removed the shade so the bare bulb is exposed) in order to blind the monster if it returns via the secret hideout. I continue the line to the bucket, which I balance on top of my door, in case the monster returns that way. If so, the bucket will fall, also tripping the lamp and blinding the monster, giving me time to respond. Yeah, I watch a lot of cartoons.

Room booby-trapped, I clutch my baseball bat and crawl into bed, keeping watch next to Watson. No way the monster can get in or out without me knowing.

CHAPTER 17

Soggy sandpaper.

That's what Watson's tongue feels like on my cheek. Too groggy to open my eyes, I push him off of me. "All right, all right, I'm getting up."

I sit on the edge of my bed and rub the sleep from my eyes. The magic stand is in place, and my room door is still ajar with the bucket balanced on top. Another night without a monster sighting should be a good thing, but I feel like a failure. A silent fart bomb detonates, stinking up the room.

"Oh, Watson. No more Snausages for you."

The hound insists it wasn't him, and I believe it because he usually sniffs his own butt after he cuts one, but it wasn't me either. I pluck my jeans off the floor and take a whiff. Fresh. Well, fresh enough. So what reeks like only a Snausage fart can?

Still seated on my bed, I bend over and peer through my legs to check underneath for maggot-infested leftovers or a decomposing carcass—that's how bad the stench is—and find nothing but the resident dust bunnies. I'm about to shrug it off to a broken sewage pipe when I notice my Vans on the other side of the bed.

The Vans.

Both of them, and they shift.

I leap up, spinning around, and shocked into paralysis, absorb it all at once.

Eight feet of ugly. Eight feet of revolting. Eight feet of pure fright. Its gigantic frame of wrinkly flesh is splotched with patches of matted fur or hair, mostly blacks and browns with streaks of orange like a brindle pattern. Its nostrils flare and release, opening wide and closing to nearly invisible slits. But scariest of all, its humanlike eyes stare into mine, calculatingly, as a string of viscous yellow drool hangs from its mouth. It snarls, revealing those jagged teeth.

Adrenaline rockets me into warp speed. I trip the lamp, blinding myself, and stumble for the door, tipping the bucket of water over my own head. Watson makes it out of the room before me and keeps going. Drenched, I pull the door shut, holding it with two slippery hands, and one soaked foot on the wall.

"Kyle!" I yell his name like I'm being murdered, but it gets him up here pronto. I don't give him a chance to speak. "The monster. In my room."

I throw open the door.

Son of a beachcomber!

It's gone. Room empty. Doesn't even stink anymore.

Kyle shakes his head sympathetically. "This is for your own good," he says, and calls down the stairs. "Dad. Monty's seeing monsters again, and now he's showering in his pajamas."

He bails, leaving me to face the monster alone. Meaning Dad.

I march into my room, growling. How is this possible? I

know I saw it. And smelled it. I plunk down on my bed, holding in a scream of frustration, and towel dry my hair with a T-shirt.

Dad rushes in and shrinks in despair at the sight of me. "Oh, Monty . . ." He eyes the bucket on the wet floor and the wire connected to the shadeless living room lamp. "What happened?"

"Just leave me alone."

"Talk to me. What's going on?"

"Nothing. I spilled some water, okay?" I'm not going to tell him about the monster. He already doesn't believe me.

He sits next to me on the bed. "I know you're having a hard time now, but it will get better. I promise."

"Yeah, you're full of promises. Promise you won't work so much, promise we won't move all the time, promise Mom will be okay—" My own emotion cuts me off. I grab my clothes from the floor and hasten for the stairs.

CHAPTER 18

Outside, Ripper waits at the end of my walkway.

I jump on my board and skate past like he doesn't exist. He falls in beside me, saying, "What's the rush?"

That's it. I jump off my board. "You wanna fight? Let's fight."

I'm so angry—at everything, the monster, Dad, life—I think I can take him.

"Dude. Chill," he says, as if he forgot he's been bullying me since I got here.

"What do you want, Ripper?" *To ambush me on the way to school? Steal my homework?* (Joke's on him, I didn't do it.) I hop on my board, but he tags alongside me.

"Just trying to be nice, that's all."

"Tell it to the Full of Crap Club."

His fake smile sours into pursed lips, confirming he had something wicked up his sleeve. "You should be happy I'm even talking to you," he says. "I determine who's in and who's out around here."

"Whatever."

A sharp whistle gets my attention. It was meant to. Zippy

and Elmo give me a nod from the gates of Crampus, which I interpret as *Get over here.*

With a smirk, I turn back to Ripper. "Should I tell them they need your approval?" I skate off and meet up with them, feeling good about finally getting the last word with a bully.

We hit Bob's Arcade—me, Zippy, and Elmo—which is swarming with high schoolers skipping class. The way everyone treats Ripper at Glen Witch is the way everyone treats Zippy and Elmo here. Respect and a little bit of fear. It spills onto me, and for once, I know what it's like to belong to the cool crowd.

As I'm about to defeat the mother ship in *Galaga Assault*, marveling at how glorious life can be, I'm hoisted up by an arm around my waist and yanked out of my (rare) joyous mood.

What the—*Dad?*

He hauls me away like a sack of kibble, and everyone in the arcade laughs, including Zippy and Elmo. If you think you can't feel color, you haven't been truly humiliated. Red hurts.

Soon as my feet hit the ground outside, I attack. "How dare you. Tracking my phone is an invasion of privacy. You have no right."

"No right? Let me remind you that I'm the father in this relationship, and I have every right to track your every move." Dad takes my hand like I'm a child and pulls me toward Glen Witch. "But I did no such thing because I thought we shared a trust with one another."

What? If he didn't track me . . .

"Doctor Petrovic's grandson saw you leave with some older boys and was concerned you'd get in trouble again for skipping school."

Agh, that weasel! My insides boil. The bully always wins. When is it my turn?

"I'm very disappointed in you, Monty. I'm sorry to say

you've lost my trust." He finally releases my hand, but holds his out, palm up. "Phone."

I relinquish it, and he goes into my settings.

"*Now* I'm tracking you." He gives me back my phone. "You're grounded, obviously. Straight home from school. And save the sarcasm."

Whatever.

We walk in silence until we reach the steps of Glen Witch, and then he turns to me, looking remorseful. He was never good at being a disciplinarian. "Running away from your problems doesn't solve anything, Monty."

"Tell that to yourself."

Dad's thrown. It takes him a beat to recover. "I'm right here, son. I'm not running anywhere."

"Really? Then why do you work so much? Why do we move every six months?"

Dad—genius scientist—has no answer. Like he didn't notice the last two years of his life since Mom died.

The bell rings.

"I gotta go unless you want me to miss second period too."

He releases me, and I hurry in but keep an even lower-than-normal profile the rest of the day. The most I can hope for is that Ripper doesn't know whether or not he got me in trouble.

A college-aged girl I've never seen before greets me with a "Hello, Montague" as soon as I get home.

"Who're you?"

"Your babysitter," she says.

Babysitter? *BABY* . . . sitter?

Dad emerges from the kitchen with Watson on his heels,

which means he was cooking. *Could this day get any worse?*

"I see you met Becky," he says with a smile.

"Why is she here?"

"I have to work tonight."

"So? What else is new?"

"I don't want you home alone."

"I'm almost thirteen, Dad. I can take care of myself."

"Monty, the last time you were home alone, you thought Godzilla was after you."

"I wasn't serious."

"You ran all the way to the university in a state of utter panic. You booby-trapped your room and ended up dumping a bucket of water on your own head because you thought you saw it again."

"Why don't you just tweet it so everyone in this stupid neighborhood can make fun of me?" I run up the stairs faster than Watson can follow, but he catches up by the third floor when I fall back against the wall, chest heaving.

"The tuna casserole's cooling on the counter," I hear Dad tell Becky. "But it's okay if he doesn't come down to eat. He usually has food in his room. Please check on him periodically, though, to make sure he's okay."

"Don't worry, Doctor Hyde. No monsters will get him on my watch." She's not laughing but her tone is.

I race up to the attic and slam my door loud enough to send a message. We'll see who has the last laugh.

CHAPTER 19

Helmet, goggles, backpack, pepper spray.

Check.

The bare bulb over the lab table is on again, casting an orange glow. I take that to mean the monster is here or has been recently. Last time, the light was off.

I tread carefully, not wanting to step on a finger or ear. Aka, crumbs. But there's no trace of blood or guts. In fact, the cellar looks the way I left it. If the monster does live down here, at least it picks up after itself.

I remove some rope and a king-sized sheet from my backpack and tuck them next to the OXIC crate. The plan: lure, spray, sheet, rope. Monster snagged. The lure, of course, Oreos.

I peel open the package and place it on the lab table, then duck behind the crates to ambush the monster. I also have my phone at the ready to snap proof because adults are picky that way. Other than the distant drone of the TV coming through the walls from the living room, it's silent. Eerily so.

For half an hour.

And then a bloodcurdling scream jolts me to my feet.

Becky! There's scrambling, more screaming, but muffled this time, struggling grunts, and footsteps running. It's got Becky.

I race to the grate, through the passageway, up the rope ladder, into my room, down the stairs to the third, then second, then main floor. Breathless, heart pounding.

The front door is wide open.

"Becky?"

A cold wind howls.

"Becky?" I lean forward to peer out and—

"Yaagghh!" a voice shouts.

I stumble back, shocked, falling off the landing of the foyer and onto my butt.

Ripper! Was he waiting to jump out and scare me?

He cracks up like it's the funniest thing he's seen. Ella's with him, looking more perplexed than anything else, and I remember I'm wearing my helmet and goggles. I yank them off but the damage is done.

"What do you want?" I say, humiliated like always.

"Your dog's outside," he says.

"Whimpering," Ella adds. "I tried to get him to come back to the house, but he won't budge."

I hurry past them to find Watson on the front lawn trembling. I hug him. "It's okay. It's nothing. I got it." He can tell I'm lying, because he doesn't stop shaking.

Reluctantly, I turn to Ripper and Ella. "Thanks," I say, even though it doesn't flow easily.

"What's wrong with him?" Ella asks.

"He must've got spooked, that's all."

"From what?" Ripper asks in a prying, not caring, way.

"Is he scared of the wind?" Ella says.

"Yeah. Wind." Well, I'm not going to tell them there's a

monster. That ate my babysitter. Three things wrong with that scenario. Monster. Ate. Babysitter.

"The wind?" Ripper doesn't buy it. "It's barely blowing."

Watson skitters away from me, frightened, and flees inside the house. Immediately, I deduce the monster's behind me and spin with my hands poised to karate chop it. Ripper snickers. It's not the monster, but close. It's that creepy Dr. Petrovic on a bright-orange Vespa. He jumps the curb and cuts the motor, parking on the sidewalk. On the back of his scooter is a rabbit in a cage.

"Archibald," the doctor says with a lopsided grin.

"Grandpa," Ripper complains. "I told you not to call me that."

"Yes, yes, whatever you want, Archibald." Dr. Petrovic turns his smile to me now. "Is he being nice to you, Montague? Be honest. Don't be shy. Speak up, son, I can't read minds."

So that's what Ripper, uh, Archibald, was trying to do this morning. Be nice. Per his grandfather's directives. He's not very good at it (and I doubt he snitched on me for my benefit), but I guess it's better than getting beaten up. "Yeah, sure."

"C'mon," Ripper says to Ella, pulling her with him as he leaves.

"Later, skater," she throws back at me. I'm sad to see half of them go.

"You shouldn't experiment on animals," I tell the doctor. "It's cruel."

"Experiment on animals? Good heavens, why would I experiment on animals when humans are much more illuminating?" He laughs uproariously, and I can't tell if he's joking.

"What's that, then?" I point to the rabbit.

He jumps excitedly and retrieves the cage. "I was told you

do magic tricks. Every magician needs a rabbit to pull out of his hat, does he not?"

I don't know what his motives are, but cool. An adorable, fluffy white rabbit with a black splotch on its left eye. "Thanks." I take the cage, already settled on the name Orville.

"Now, do tell me about your monster, Montague. Please. Tell me everything."

I look up, optimistic. "My monster?"

"Yes, Montague. Your monster. That I presume is not Godzilla."

Finally. Someone believes me. Wait. Of course the weirdo does. I have enough problems without Pastrami Breath hanging around. "Oh, you mean the *friend* I made?"

"Indeed. Indeed!"

"It's someone I met at the arcade. You know, typical bully. Everyone thinks he's a monster."

Dr. Petrovic's jubilant expression snaps to stone, and he glowers at me with a ruthlessness that sends chills down my arms. "Cross your heart, hope to die, stick a ten-inch needle in your eye?"

"Huh?"

"On your mother's grave, Montague. Are you being truthful? Or are you a liar? A fibber? Deceiver?"

"Monty," Kyle calls out, jogging over from Diego's house, and I exhale a nervous titter of relief. "What're you doing outside? Where's the sitter?"

"I don't know. She took off."

"Why? What'd you do?"

"*I* didn't do anything."

"I'll see him in," Dr. Petrovic says, plucking a hair from my head.

"Ow. Did you just—"

"Thanks, doc, but I got it." Kyle pushes me inside and slams the door in Dr. Petrovic's face.

I turn back to make sure the ghoul leaves, and witness his eye pop out of its socket. Like, hanging from a string. I clutch my stomach before it articulates what I'm thinking all over the foyer.

The doc shoves his eye back in, muttering, and walks away. I'm too stunned to say anything to Kyle, who is busy blaming me for Becky's departure and threatening to stop covering for me with Dad. As if I'm always getting into trouble.

CHAPTER 20

New plan.

I hole up in the closet where I can see everything that goes on in my room through the slats.

I've made a dummy of myself with pillows and tucked it under the bedcovers. Rigged to the ceiling is a large fishing net (also courtesy of Dad's one-time fishing expedition) connected to a rip cord, which I hold on to tightly.

"Let's see you fake me out this time."

Sunlight bleeds through my closed eyelids.

Watson's licking my face. Incessantly. "All right already, Watson."

I swipe his tongue away and struggle to open my eyes. Morning always gets here too soon. It's not until the slats come into focus that I remember where I am. In my closet.

Squinting, I peer out and see Watson staring back at me from the other side.

"Watson?"

Then who was licking my face?

I turn to find the eight-foot-tall monster hunched among my tees and empty hangers. I run. And slam into the closet door so hard fireworks go off in my head.

The wet slobbery tongue licks my cheek.

This time I jump back as I come to, wiping my face— "Gross!"—and discover I'm in the middle of my room. No denying it: the ugly, fleshy, patchy-haired monster (and owner of that slobbery tongue) is right there. For the reals. It must get some sort of kick playing with its food, because it could've eaten me (and Watson and Orville) while I was passed out.

I eye the fishing net overhead, in perfect position. Problem is, the rip cord is on the other side of the monster. I grab the closest weapon in reach—my wand from the magic stand—and poke the air between us. "Don't come any closer. I'm warning you."

The monster takes the wand and, with a flick of its wrist, turns it into a bouquet of flowers.

"Seriously? Everyone but me?"

"Monty, let's get a move on," Dad calls from the third floor, startling me and the monster.

I recover first and dive for the rip cord, pulling it as I yell, "Dad, c'mere. Quick!"

When I turn back, Watson is trapped under the net and the monster is gone.

"Ugggghhh. Never mind!" This monster is infuriating. I pluck my jeans off the magic stand to get dressed, and the monster explodes out of the top like an *Alien* chest burst!

Aaaaaghhhh.

I flee, pulling the netted Watson with me to save his life too. Slung over my shoulder, the load bangs against the back of my legs with every step, punctuated by a grunt or groan coming from one or both of us—I don't even know—but I don't stop until I race all the way into the kitchen.

Dad and Kyle are battling over a waffle in the toaster, each with a hand on it.

"Dad, I got the monster."

"That's Watson," Dad says, looking at the netted dog. I roll my eyes.

"No. Not here. In my room. It hides, that's why you've never seen—" Hold everything. Kyle's wearing jeans. "Where's your skirt?"

"I lent it to Crystal. Well, I completed my pledge. It's not like I need it anymore. I mean, it's a skirt, right? It's just a skirt. Get off my back." Kyle storms out.

Okay.

"Dad, are you coming?" I run back upstairs at full speed, and the un-netted Watson keeps pace. Dad runs like a forty-something-year-old. Slow. But I keep going. He'll catch up eventually.

I throw open the door and, as predicted, no monster. But I know its tricks now. I flip open the top on the magic stand and, "Ha!"

Not there.

In the closet? Nope. Under the bed? No such luck. Behind the curtains? *Come on!*

Dad finally makes it in, panting. "Is it here?"

"Well, do you see it?"

He looks around. "Um . . ."

"Forget it." I get dressed.

"It's not that I don't believe you, Monty."

"Then what? Do you or don't you?"

"I believe you *think* you see a monster."

"Just leave."

"Monty," Dad says, taking my hand, and I know I'm in for it. "Losing a parent is traumatic—"

"Stop. This has nothing to do with Mom."

"Okay," Dad says, releasing my hand. "Okay." He kisses my forehead and leaves.

I swing the door shut after him. Not everything has to be about the most terrible thing that ever happened to you.

I dive facedown on my bed, head hanging over the edge, and that's when I notice Orville's cage bulging with a fleshy, splotchy hairball. Two big brown eyes pop open and stare at me. It's the monster. Stuffed in the cage.

I spring to my feet, arm pointing like I'm in charge. "Get out of there now."

Incredibly, the thing squeezes its ginormous body through the cage door and pops back into perfect shape. If I didn't see it with my own eyes, I'd say it was impossible, but I've got bigger problems than trying to figure out what's normal for a monster.

It's got my sweet little Orville by the scruff, sniffing it with its hideous fleshy nostrils. Eyes narrowed, the monster opens its saliva-dripping mouth, exposing razor-sharp teeth.

"No!"

The monster freezes, mouth wide open. Its eyes dart back and forth, from me to the bunny, me to the bunny, me to the bunny. As if there's a decision to be made.

I hold out my hand, palm up. "Release the rabbit."

After one more glance between the two of us, the monster drops Orville into my hand. *Thank you.* We stare each other down until I remember you're not supposed to look a wild animal in the eye, so I drop my gaze. Don't run, either; they'll chase you. What do I do, what do I do?

Moving very slowly, I take three giant steps back. It charges, snarling rabidly and frothing at the mouth. *Ack!* I curl into a ball, shielding Orville, but the monster brushes past us and tears into my backpack. It pulls out a Snickers and shoves the entire thing, wrapper and all, in its mouth.

Imperceptibly fast, its face changes from threatening to gentle. The narrow eyes soften into innocent orbs, the fleshy nostrils calm and almost disappear, and the fangs retreat behind pouty lips. The monster pats down its matted hair and looks at me guiltily.

Are you for real?

It burps, putting me and Kyle to shame, and a chortle slips out of me. It's not aggressive, it's hungry. In fact, it's not even that scary now that I scrutinize it. Sure, it reeks like rotten cabbage, and true, it's not cuddly cute, but scary? Not really.

"Hang on," I tell it. I deposit Orville in the cage and ransack my dresser for my secret stash of Oreos. The package is shredded to smithereens, not a crumb left. "Hey. Did you—"

"Monty?" Dad calls. "Come down for breakfast."

The monster makes a dash for the door, but I'm one step ahead and block the exit. "No you don't. That's my family. You can't eat them."

The monster bats its long lashes—*doink, doink*—and shakes its head, like it would never.

"Right. As if." People aren't vanishing for no reason. "Make you a deal. I'll let you have my breakfast if you promise to stay here."

The monster's eyes light up.

"You understand?"

It nods emphatically.

"Really? You promise to stay put?"

The monster makes a show of planting its feet firmly on the floor.

Imagine that. It understands.

He. Understands.

CHAPTER 21

Communicating with Your Teenager.

Dad's got the book half-hidden behind his back, but I recognize the corner of the cover. This time, it might work in my favor.

"Dad, about the monster . . ."

"I'm all ears, Monty. I'm ready to *hear* what you're saying."

It's hard not to roll my eyes. "Well, he's back."

He looks around the kitchen.

"Will you stop that? You know he's not here. Do you see him?"

"I'm sorry. Go on."

"He's real, Dad. I talked to him. He's friendly."

"He is? What did he say?"

"Well, he doesn't talk. But he understands."

"I see. And hear you. There's a friendly monster, not here but somewhere in the house, who can understand you, but he can't talk."

"Exactly."

"Okay, I'm with you so far. Do you think I can meet him?"

"Probably, but he's kinda timid for a monster. That's why he hides all the time. So you have to promise to be nice."

"Of course. I merely want to say hello and make sure he's healthy. After all, we don't want to expose ourselves to Franken-pneumonia."

That's Dad's attempt at a joke, but I don't like what it implies. "You're not gonna go all scientist on him, are you?"

"Monty, if there's a monster—"

"If?"

"Calm down, son. All I meant is *any* monster in the house needs to be tested for diseases."

"You mean dissected."

"Of course not. You know dissections are only performed on the dead."

"Dead?"

"Monty, I promise I won't dissect your monster."

Yeah, when was the last time you kept a promise? "Actually, I'm not a hundred percent sure what I saw was a monster. In fact, the more I think about it, the more I think it was shadows." I throw in a laugh to sell it. "Yeah. Shadows. Spooky."

Dad's brow furrows with concern. "I'm listening. Go on."

"That's it. The end." I grab a box of Pop-Tarts. "Starving. Forgot my books upstairs. Back down in a sec." I take off.

When I throw open the door to my room, Watson's backed into a corner, far away from the monster, who has two rabbit ears sticking out of his mouth.

"Holy turd balls!" I spring into action, pulling Orville from his mouth. Astonishingly, stringy slobber is the only damage. I spin to the monster, furious.

"Did you not understand me before? Orville's not for eating. I don't care how hungry you get. Is Watson next?"

Watson flees.

"Am I?"

Lips trembling, the monster vanishes, *poof*, in a ghostly trail. And I'm left staring into thin air, shocked. "Hello? Monster?"

He doesn't surface.

"Are you here?"

Not a peep.

Sensitive.

Sacrificing one of my tees, I wipe the saliva off Orville and put him back in the cage. I wait a beat to see if the monster will return, but he doesn't.

"I'm sorry, okay? I didn't mean to yell, it's just— "

Wham! The monster bursts out of the closet, sending me stumbling back from fright, clutching my heart.

"Don't do that!"

He giggles.

"Yeah, hilarious. You're a real master of illusion, aren't you, disappearing and reappearing all the time. A monster Houdini."

Doink, doink.

"Oh, you like that? Then that's what I'm gonna call you. Houdini."

The monster licks my face from my cheek to my hair, which now stands straight up, thanks to the gummy spit.

"Ugh." I grab the contaminated tee to wipe off. "In case you didn't get it the first time, guh-ross."

He comes at me again, and I'm caught between trying to take cover and push him away.

"Ew. Stop," I say through laughter. His bristly tongue tickles, and his breath smells like eggs boiled in sewer water. I manage to squirm out of reach and jump on his back, but before I can tackle him to the ground, Dad calls me.

"Monty, let's go. You're late."

Houdini bolts upright, but I'm quick to say, "Don't get any ideas. My family's off-limits. That includes pets." I release my grip and jump to the floor. "Understood?"

He grumbles and nods.

"I'm serious."

He nods emphatically.

"Thank you." I throw my backpack over my shoulder and head for the door, then turn back. "And stay here till I get back. I mean it."

He folds his arms and pouts.

"I'm sorry, but that's the way it's got to be until I can figure things out." Reluctantly, I leave.

CHAPTER 22

School is a blur.

I have monster on the brain, and a gazillion ways things have surely gone wrong. In my gym shorts—I didn't take up precious seconds to slip my regular clothes over them like I normally do—I skate for home posthaste. When I sail through the gates of Crampus, I'm relieved there are no signs of carnage.

I tear into the house, race up to the attic, throw open the door, and—"Agh!"—trip over something or other as soon as I enter. I belly flop onto the floorboards, knocking the wind (from both ends) out of me. But I saw enough on the way down to rocket me to my feet in an instant.

"What the *how*?"

Our massive stainless-steel double-door refrigerator is in the middle of my room. That's not what I tripped over, though. Next to the fridge is our dining table and two chairs. Also, not what tripped me. It's the bags and bags of groceries that did me in. Ill-gotten goods from our pantry. Empty wrappers, cans, and food packaging litter the place like a tornado aftermath with Watson amidst it. He wags his tail but doesn't get off his over-indulged butt to come over and greet me.

My bed has been tipped upright, leaning against the wall, to make room for all this stuff. And now my pillow and blankets comingle with the resident dust bunnies.

"Houdini?"

A mound of dirty laundry erupts, raining tees and underwear, as Houdini pops out from within. A pair of tighty-whities lands on my head.

"Houdini, why?"

He plunks me in the chair, dumps a shopping bag of snacks on the table, and takes a seat opposite me. I grab his hand as he reaches for a box of graham crackers. "No. All this has to go back downstairs before Dad or Kyle gets home."

Brow pinched in confusion, he motions back and forth between us.

"I'm sorry. We can't eat our meals together. Not at the table, anyway."

Why? he pantomimes with his hands up by his shoulders.

"Because Dad will notice it's missing, and then he'll find out about you. And trust me, you don't want him to find out."

Houdini dives into the magic stand to show me how swiftly he can hide.

"I get it. You can disappear." He pops up, nodding. "But having this stuff up here is a dead giveaway. Now help me put it back."

I grab three bags of groceries in a bear hug, and Houdini does the same with the refrigerator. The front door slams shut, and I freeze. Houdini too. "Someone's home," I whisper.

Footsteps jog up the stairs, and I drop the bags, spinning full circle, panicked. Houdini releases the fridge and zips behind the curtains to hide. I grab my blanket and throw it over the fridge as if it might be a homemade fort.

The footsteps stop on the second story as Kyle calls up. "Monty?"

"What?"

"I'll be at Diego's. Dad says there's lasagna in the fridge."

Houdini peeks out from behind the curtain and shakes his head no. I roll my eyes.

" 'Kay. Bye," I yell down, thankful he's too self-concerned to notice the dining room table is not in the dining room. I run to the window, push Houdini out of the way, and watch until Kyle goes inside Diego's house. "Let's go."

I grab the three bags again. Houdini beats me to the door, carrying the fridge, and lopes down the stairs. By the time I reach the second floor, he's on his way back up. He passes me again on his way down, this time with the table and chairs.

"Meet you back in my room," I tell him as I head into the kitchen to restock the pantry. I unload the bags lickety-split and jet back upstairs.

When I return to my room, Houdini's gazing out the window longingly. I join him to see Ella, Ripper, Thrash, and the other guy (whose name I still don't know) hanging out in front of Ella's house with their boards. Thrash and the other guy are doing some tricks on the curb while Ripper and Ella chat on her porch steps.

Houdini holds up one of my skateboards and, with a huge smile, points to the outside.

"Sorry, Houdini, can't. If anyone sees you, it's over."

Pouting, he trudges to the corner and plops on the floor. I know that look. Boredom.

"Tell you what. When everyone's asleep, we'll sneak out."

He shoots upright. *SQUEE!*

"Shhh. I said sneak, not announce it to the world."

Squee.

Hot, sticky sardine breath wakes me up.

Doink. Doink.

Ugh. I push Houdini out of my face. "Go away."

He rolls me off the bed and onto the floor.

"Houdini." I look at the clock. "It's two in the morning."

He nods excitedly and shoves the board onto my chest.

"But it's two in the morning."

He nods again and points to the outside.

Sigh. Me and my big ideas. "Skateboards make too much noise for the middle of the night," I say, placing it next to the others. "But we can go out."

Houdini claps his hands silently. Yawning, I put on yesterday's jeans and tee, and slip into my tennies, sockless. I leave Watson behind my closed bedroom door and gently tiptoe down the stairs, gesturing for Houdini to do the same.

Outside, the crispness of night energizes me. Houses are dark except for porch lights. The streets are scary-movie quiet, but I'm not afraid because I'm the one with the monster.

I lead Houdini to the park in Crampus. Even though it technically closes at sundown, there aren't any locks to keep you out, only on the gates to the skate park. Houdini squeals and races to the swing set. It's the kind with the belt seat hanging by chains, and it's definitely not meant for giants.

"Wait," I say, running after, but Houdini hops onto the swing, butt first, and the chain breaks. He hits the ground with a shocked expression.

I muffle a laugh and help him to his feet. "What'd you expect? The playground's for little kids."

He points to me.

"I'm not a little kid."

He gives me the *really?* look as he motions to his height then down to mine.

"Well, everyone's little compared to you. Hey, wait. You can make yourself small like when you got into Orville's cage. Do that."

Eyes wide with delight, he inhales a dramatically huge breath, and inflates like a Macy's Thanksgiving Day parade balloon.

"Smaller, not bigger."

When he's sure to burst, he exhales powerfully, sending swings swinging and branches flailing and the merry-go-round spinning. As his lungs empty, he shrinks all the way down to a kid-sized monster.

"You look funny."

You do, he retorts by pointing to me.

"No, you do." We shove each other a couple of times for fun, and then he hops on a swing, wriggling with joy.

"Hold on tight." I place his hands around the chains and give him a push from behind. He looks over his shoulder at me, smiling from molar to molar. I push him higher. And higher. Back and forth and *BOOF!* He pops to his regular size as I'm about to push again, knocking me off my feet. *SNAP* goes the chain, and Houdini lands on top of me. Chortling, he rolls off.

"Nice. Squash the guy who's only doing everything for you."

He gasps, affronted I'd suggest he did it on purpose.

"Well then, what happened? You can't stay small?"

He shakes his head and wipes his sweaty brow.

"Oh, I see. It takes effort. That's okay. I like you big, anyway."

He motions to me and lowers his hand to indicate he likes me small.

"I told you, I'm not—oh, never mind. Tag, you're it!" I tap his arm and take off running. He catches on and chases me. Since we have the entire park to ourselves, I crisscross all the different fields. Even though Houdini can cover more ground faster than me, I can spin, dodge, and change directions faster than him. It's a fair game, and we spend hours tagging and trying to outrun each other.

After that, we ride the merry-go-round. Thanks to Houdini pushing this time, the world smears past at supersonic speed. Eventually, we both wobble off, unable to walk straight, and tumble to the ground, laughing. It's only staring at the sky that I realize it's almost morning. I jump to my feet. "We gotta go."

CHAPTER 23

No surprise, I slept through most of my classes today.

I don't think any of my teachers will tell Dad since they all reprimanded me on the spot. I skate through the gates of Crampus, eager to flop on my bed and catch some Zs.

"How's your chicken?" Ripper says from behind me. Perfect.

"I don't have a chicken."

"Sure you do. Long ears. Droopy eyes. Scared of the wind."

I don't engage further, and Ripper goes his way, and I continue on mine. As I turn onto my walkway from the sidewalk, Kyle bolts from the house, alarming me.

"What's up, everything okay, anything unusual?" I blurt out.

"You're the only unusual thing around here," he says, sprinting down the street. His insult is a relief. He must just be late for a class.

I hurry in, greet Watson with some belly rubs, and run up to the attic. Watson follows. I presume Houdini will be front and center when I enter, or at least emerge from some bizarre hiding place, but he's nowhere around.

"Houdini?"

He doesn't surface.

That's strange. I check behind the curtains. Not there.

"Houdini?"

Nothing. Now I'm starting to get that tingling sensation of adrenaline.

"I'm serious, Houdini. Where are you?" My room is way too quiet and un-smelly for me to remain calm. I shove aside the trapdoor and scramble down to my secret hideout. It, too, is devoid of stinky, hairy life. Anxiety shoots from zero to ten as I race back to my room with awful scenarios in my mind. Did he run away? Is he on a rampage? Is he dead?

Not knowing what else to do, I gather a handful of loose strands off the floor for Watson to smell. "Find Houdini, Watson. Find Houdini."

Watson sniffs the fuzz and trots off, nose to the ground. He goes directly to the front door, which I open for him, and continues to the sidewalk. I follow, chewing my lip, eyes darting every which way. The neighborhood is crowded with people—on front lawns, in cars, walking dogs, jogging—but no one looks like they've seen an eight-foot-tall monster.

Block by block, I call out his name in a whisper and get no response. Watson's nose takes us to the park behind the university, and I realize he's been following last night's trail.

"Crickets," I say, kicking the sod in disappointment.

Watson looks at me with worried eyes—he hates when I curse—but I pat his head to reassure him. "Sorry, Watson. Everything's fine. You did good."

But where's Houdini?

———

"I said let's go, Monty. It's seven forty-five."

Huh? What?

Dad retreats down the stairs, leaving my bedroom door open.

I wipe the crusty saliva off my chin. Last thing I remember, it was three in the morning and Houdini still hadn't come home. My body shakes with fatigue, but I force myself to sit up. I wait a second for the wooziness to pass, then reach for my jeans on the floor. Houdini's big brown eyes stare at me from under the bed. I jump up. "Houdini."

He hops up in front of me, all smiles, but I'm not having it.

"Where were you?"

He motions to outside.

"Yeah, der. Do you know what you put me through? I thought something happened to you, something terrible. You're not allowed to go outside without me. You got that?"

He gazes down, eyes drooped in sorrow.

"Yeah, you should feel bad. I was worried sick. What if someone saw you?"

He shakes his head, implying he wasn't seen.

"This time. But you might not be so lucky next time. You have to promise you won't go anywhere without me. Got it?"

He nods.

"I'm serious."

He nods.

"Not joking."

He nods more emphatically.

"Okay." I hug him, and he squeezes me so hard, I toot. We both giggle.

CHAPTER 24

Stink . . . y.

"Do you smell that?" Dad asks, sniffing the air.

Martians can smell that.

Only one thing reeks that bad, but Houdini promised he wouldn't go out without me. *Gasp.* I realize my mistake. *Without me.* And here I am. Is he clever enough to defy me on a technicality? I don't see him anywhere, though. Only students filing toward Glen Witch. His odor most likely rubbed off on my clothes. Yeah. That's it. I make a mental note to teach him personal hygiene. I've got enough flaws without eau de monster as my scent.

"They must be cleaning the septic tanks," Dad says, which saves me the embarrassment of confessing to an upset stomach.

"You don't have to keep taking me to school, you know."

"Thanks, but I don't want any more texts from your principal."

"So change your number."

Dad sighs. "Honestly, Monty."

Ella passes us on her board, throwing me an over-the-shoulder smirk. *Fantastic.* 1) She witnesses me being walked to school, and 2) she probably thinks I farted that stench into the air.

"Come on, Dad. Everyone makes fun of me already."

"In the spirit of rebuilding our trust and to show you I'm on your side, you can continue on your own. But I'm going to watch until you enter the building."

It's a start. I take off, embracing the freedom, and pull a spectacular Caballerial kickflip.

Fur. Flesh. *Agh!*

Amazingly, I don't wipe out, but I saw it midflip: the underside of my deck covered in matted fur-hair. I pop the board up, and sure enough, two big brown eyes stare at me.

Houdini *did* get me on a technicality.

I hug the board to my chest and glance over my shoulder. Dad waves. I wave back and run up the stairs and inside. Immediately, I'm accosted with insults, but who can blame them?

"Take a shower."

"Deodorant, dude."

"My eyes. They burn."

Lots of laughter.

Sweat fires out of every pore on my body. Ducked by the door, I peek outside. Dad's heading away. When he rounds the corner, I jet out of the school, carrying my board. Next thing I know, Houdini's running alongside me.

Jeezy Creezy! "What're you doing? You can't let anyone see— "

"Yo, kid."

Busted! I freeze.

Zippy and Elmo emerge from around the side of the school building.

"Uh . . . Monty," Zippy remembers, and I wonder why no

one's saying anything about the huge monster next to me.

He's gone, that's why. The way he always disappears.

"You gotta do us a favor," Zippy says.

"I can't. I have to get to school."

They laugh. "No, really," Elmo says, and they continue down the street expecting me to follow.

"But I have a test today," I lie.

Zippy turns back. "I thought you were our friend, man."

"I am."

"Then prove it."

There you have it. The cost of having friends. I glance around one more time, but if Houdini is nearby, I can't see (or smell) him. As I'm about to follow Zippy and Elmo, an outburst of barking erupts in the pet store across the street, and my heart surges. I wait for people to run out, screaming. Instead, the barking stops abruptly. OMG. Did my monster devour the entire store?

Elmo flicks an extinguished cigarette butt at me to get my attention. "Let's go."

Twenty minutes later, we're in a part of town I've never been in before and hope to never be in again. Apartment buildings are covered in graffiti but not the nice kind. Mostly names over names, competing with each other until none are legible. Bars protect every first-floor window on the street. We pass a corner liquor store, and Elmo darts in, but Zippy keeps going, so I do too.

Elmo catches up to us by the time we reach an alley that cuts through the block. "Snickers?" He tosses the chocolate bar to me, then flips a cigarette in his mouth.

"We got some business to take care of," Zippy says. "All you gotta do is whistle if you see a cop. Okay?"

What? No. Not okay! Please let me leave. "Okay."

Smiling, he pats me on the back, and he and Elmo make their way down the alley where another guy waits.

"Oh, this isn't good," I mutter as I stare at my shoes. Then I remember I'm supposed to be keeping watch. I scan up and down the street. No cops. I turn my attention back to the alley where Elmo hands over money and the guy gives him a small package. I turn away quickly. I can't be a witness too. It's bad enough to be the lookout.

As I study the dirty graffiti pondering what I got myself into, I'm shoved into the wall from behind. Before I can protest—I assume it's Houdini roughhousing—I hear, "Police. Freeze." There's running, yelling, scuffling, but I can't see what's going on. A hand keeps me pressed against the paint.

If anyone asked me a day ago what would be worse than a monster on the loose, I'd say nothing. Today, the answer is cops.

CHAPTER 25

Kyle drags me into the house by my wrist.

It's not that I'm fighting him, I just can't keep up with his six-foot-tall strides. Other than calling Glen Witch to cover for me with an unnecessarily graphic story about food poisoning coming out of both ends, he hasn't spoken since we left the police station. I got the scared-straight lecture from a sergeant who said I was fortunate to be a first-time offender (clearly unaware of my previous school-ditching escapade), otherwise I'd be sitting in a cell alongside other criminals. Which seems preferable to my current situation.

Watson knows a bubbling volcano when he sees one and doesn't approach. Kyle slams the door, and I can't help but mutter, "Man, you're cranky since you started wearing pants again."

Still holding me by the wrist, he spins me around so I'm in front of him, face-to-face. His usually perfect complexion is blotched with rage. He inhales deeply to calm himself, but I don't think it's working. "Do you have any idea what they were doing?" he says through a clenched jaw.

"I'm not an idiot."

"You are if you were helping."

"They're my friends, okay. Leave them alone."

"They're not your friends, Monty. They're using you."

"No, they're not."

"You think they like you? Wake up."

Ow. That one hurt. "What do you know?" I start up the stairs before tears erupt. Watson follows me.

"You're lucky I don't tell Dad," Kyle calls up.

"And you're lucky I don't tell him you were drinking beer at Diego's."

"Go ahead. We'll see which he thinks is worse."

"I would, but he's never around, is he?" I yell down as I keep climbing.

"Oh, for Pete's sake, Monty, would you give him a break, already? Dad's got feelings too, you know. He's just trying to adjust."

"For two years! Always moving. Always working. Well, what about me?"

"Me, me, me," Kyle says. "Like you're the only one making sacrifices. You think I had to go to this rinky-dink school?"

"Bull crap. If you got accepted anywhere else, you would've gone." Now we're yelling up and down three flights of stairs.

"You really are a butt-wipe, you know that?"

"Well, I must be, 'cause that seems to be my middle name around here." I slam my bedroom door, flop on my bed, and cry into my pillow. Stupid feelings. Watson licks my head to console me.

A ruckus outside that only skaters can create with ollies and kickflips and grinds tells me that school's out. Wiping my face, I roll over and find Houdini peering out of the magic stand.

"Well, if it isn't Mr. I'm-Gonna-Do-Whatever-I-Want-And-You-Can't-Stop-Me."

He climbs out of the magic stand and produces my top hat—ta-da!—like it's a trick, not like he was hiding it behind his back this whole time.

"I'm not blind. You're gonna have to do better than that."

He reaches into the hat and pulls out a rabbit.

"Hey!" I whip my eyes over to the cage, but Orville's still in there. Wait a second. "You *were* in the pet store. I knew it."

Houdini offers the new rabbit to me in his open palm, like an appetizer on a tray. This one doesn't have the dark patch of fur around its eye like Orville does. It's a pure-white cotton ball.

"Let's get one thing straight right now: no one's eating this rabbit."

Houdini shakes his head and pats the rabbit to assure me it's not food. I accept it from him, and he brightens. He pulls another rabbit out of the hat, an extra-fluffy brown-furred ball of cuteness.

"How many did you get? That's stealing, you know?"

He holds this one to his chest, rocking it the way I cuddled Watson when I first got him, and I realize Houdini wants a pet of his own. Everyone knows they're great for teaching responsibility. That's how Mom talked Dad into letting me have Watson. And there's plenty of room in Orville's cage.

"Okay, you can keep it. We'll name them Snowball and Smore." Smore because it looks like a toasted marshmallow.

Ecstatic, Houdini kisses Smore, and instantaneously, his nostrils flare, eyes narrow, and fangs protrude. He's this-close to popping that bunny in his mouth when my jarring "Houdini!" snaps him out of it.

He looks at me, head tilted in confusion. *Doink, doink.*

"For the last time, you don't eat pets. Pets are not for eating. Not mine, not yours, not anyone's, got it?"

Frowning, he rubs his stomach.

"I don't care how hungry you are. Eat dead food like the rest of us." I dig a bologna sandwich I was saving for later out of my backpack and trade it for Smore. "And I can't believe I have to say this, but no more snacking on people either."

Houdini points to himself and shakes his head no.

"Yeah, I'm acquainted with the 'not me' defense. It's called lying." I deposit both Snowball and Smore in the cage with Orville, then turn to my monster. "One more thing . . ."

Hot water steams up the bathroom.

"If we're gonna share a room, you have to lose the gnarly stench."

Houdini huddles in the corner, shoeless, whimpering for mercy.

"That doesn't work for Watson, and it's not gonna work for you." I take his hand and march to the shower, ignoring his plaintive whines. It's called tough love. But when I turn to usher him in, he's still in the corner and I've still got his hand. His arm is stretched across the entire span of the bathroom.

"Ack!" I release my grip, and incredibly, his arm recoils into perfect shape. I snuffle-chuckle in relief.

"That was awesome, Houdini. You can be all Stretch Armstrong, and it doesn't hurt?"

He rubs his arm, meaning it did hurt.

"Well, why didn't you say so?"

He throws his hands up in disbelief and imitates the plaintive whine.

"You're right. I'm sorry. I'll try to listen better."

Somehow, he interprets that as his cue to leave and grabs the knob, but I stiff-arm the door, keeping it closed. "Whoa, whoa, whoa. We're not done here. You reek like yesterday's garbage. Even you must smell it."

Houdini sniffs himself and gives the thumbs-up.

"Wrong. Reeking is bad."

No, he insists and thrusts his armpit in my nose to show me. Cut to: an onslaught of water shocking me back to consciousness.

I'm under the stream of the shower—which is the complete opposite of what's supposed to be going on here—gasping and spitting out buckets' worth.

Drenched, I trudge out of the stall and point, saying through gritted teeth, "In. Now."

Even he can't make an argument for BO that knocks someone out cold. Head hung in remorse, he squeezes into the shower. The steam wilts his coarse wire-haired coat, and he presses back against the tiles, away from the water. His bare feet are almost as long and wide as the stall. He has five plump, hairy toes on each foot, like a human, and I realize I never counted his fingers. Also five on each hand. While I'm at it, I sneak a glance (now that his fur is not fluffed out) to confirm that he's a he and not a she.

Confirmed.

"I hate to break it to you, but you have to get wet to get clean."

Still making amends for rendering me unconscious, Houdini obediently steps into the stream. Being as tall as he is, he has to crouch to get his head and whole body under the showerhead. His fur clings to him once he's soaked through, and reveals an undernourished frame.

"Houdini. You're skin and bones."

He nods.

"I'm sorry, buddy. I didn't realize how much food a guy your size needs. I'll get you some more when we're done."

He pulls me in for a sloshy hug. *Doink, doink. Snort. Squeee.*

"Of course I'll feed you," I say, extricating myself from his waterlogged chest. "Jeez, Houdini. Don't you know by now you can count on me? I'll always be there for you. We're best friends."

His bottom lip trembles with emotion, and he pulls me in again.

Note to self: go easy on the sentiment.

I finally found someone who likes tuna casserole.

Houdini scarfed it down, along with mystery stew, a loaf of sourdough bread, a block of cheddar cheese, and a carton of orange juice. It was the most I could carry in one load.

He should be good for the night, but keeping him fed so he doesn't eat anyone is going to be a challenge. The more I can learn about him, the better I can take care of him, but there's no manual on monsters. Only the *Human Replication and Reanimation* journal, and there was nothing remotely Houdini-like in any of those pages. Though there were the odd creatures in the gene-splicing section: puffer fish, mutable rainfrog, wrap-around spider, mimic octopus. I grab my phone and search the internet.

The more I read, the more it starts to make sense. Those species are known for shapeshifting abilities (which only reinforces my belief in werewolves). It's to protect themselves from predators and sometimes to get food. I bet those genes are part of that green slime, giving Houdini some of the same traits. That's how he can stretch or flatten out or scrunch into a tiny ball of fur. I feel better knowing he's got built-in survival skills, as long as he doesn't use them to trick people into being meals.

Exhausted, I climb into bed. Watson jumps up next to me, and Houdini's about to follow.

"Sorry, Houdini. There's barely enough room for Watson, and I know you can't stay small for long."

Houdini heads to the magic stand and I figure he's going to disappear like always, but I'm wrong. He puts on my cape, which barely covers his broad shoulders, and I giggle from the sight. He pantomimes the international *nothing-up-my-sleeve*, then magically produces a string of scarves tied together. I curl into my pillow to watch. A bedtime story the way Mom used to tell them.

With a flick of his wrist, Houdini parachutes a scarf over the rabbit cage.

Naturally, I'm suspicious. "What're you doing?"

He dramatically whips the scarf away. Ta-da!

Orville is gone. I shoot up, alarmed. "Houdini!"

He tosses the scarf over the cage again, but I yank it away and find Orville back among his two friends, twitching his nose as if nothing happened. Relief is my first emotion, but jealousy is a close second. I've been trying to do that for months.

"How'd you do that?"

Houdini shrugs.

Sure, sure. A magician never tells.

I climb back into bed as he moves on to his next trick. He cuts a rope in half, then ties the two halves together. My eyelids are lead, and I miss the rest of the trick. Half-asleep, I feel weight of Houdini draped across the foot of my bed like a spare blanket. Snores emit instantly, rhythmically in time with Watson.

CHAPTER 26

The squeak of my doorknob is enough to jolt me awake.

Kyle sticks his head in. "Hey."

Watson's still on the bed next to me, but Houdini's gone.

"Hey," I say back. It's our way of apologizing for our fight.

"Dad's tux is ready at the dry cleaners."

"So?"

"So pick it up."

"Why can't you do it?"

"Because last night."

Darn it. I guess I should be happy he doesn't tell Dad about my crime spree. "Fine."

Kyle leaves, and Houdini slithers out of the pillowcase, shaking off loose feathers.

"Remind me to never play hide-and-seek with you." I pull on a pair of jeans and pop the tail of my board, sending it airborne so I can catch it.

Houdini tries to copy me with another one of my boards and clocks himself in the head. I can't help but laugh even though the pink skin underneath his fur turns bright red from embarrassment.

"Tell you what. I'll teach you to skate if you show me how to make the rabbits disappear."

Houdini grabs my arm and zips out of the room, flying down the stairs. My feet never touch the ground until we're outside, in the backyard, and I'm dizzy with distress. Remarkably, I'm still clutching my board. I steel myself for Kyle to race out of the house with a baseball bat to rescue me, but he doesn't, and I'm sure we passed him along the way. In fact, I can smell the Eggo he was toasting.

Crickets! Houdini's got the waffle.

"Did you take my Eggo, butt-wipe?"

Ack. I spin to Kyle, who's yelling out the kitchen window. If he stuck his head out half an inch, he'd see Houdini flattened up against the wall with Eggo crumbs on his face.

"No. Hunh-unh. Didn't touch it." It's the truth.

Kyle retreats, and I slide a disapproving glare at Houdini. After a sheepish smile, he sticks out his tongue, offering the fully intact, albeit slobbered-upon, waffle.

"Nobody wants it now."

Thrilled, he gulps it down.

With the crisis over, I size up the backyard. Abandoned. Overgrown. A jungle gym with more jungle than gym. There's a dilapidated tree house dangling precariously from a huge oak and a rusted swing set without any swings, just chains looking for something to do. If the rotted wooden fence circling the perimeter is ours, our backyard is huge. I plod through the wild vegetation, imagining the skate park I could build here if I had a year to clear out all this brush.

"I'm glad you understand that we can't let anyone see you, Houdini, but there's nowhere to skate back here."

He yanks me with him as he takes off, and once again, my feet skim the ground, unable to stop, unable to keep up. *Whoosh!* I drop into a hole, and my heart races as rapidly as my mind. I'm plummeting down a forgotten well twenty feet deep. Or an ancient snake-infested mine shaft. Or into my own grave courtesy of the resident ax-wielding murderer. But the sidewall greets me, clipping off my scream, and I slide to the bottom, flat on my back. Unhurt. Houdini stands over me, grinning, and I see why.

We're in an empty pool.

"No way!" I jump to my feet, stoked. A pool in my own backyard.

Bone dry, littered with twigs and leaves, it's perfect. The surface, an inch below the flora, is almost smooth against my palms. There's minor chipping in spots, mostly near the faded tile by the lip of the pool, but nothing that would pose a problem.

We clear the debris in ten minutes flat. When you have a giant monster who can scoop and discard without having to climb out of the pool, it's a time-saver.

Five minutes after that, Houdini's dropping in and carving the bowl like a pro. Sure, he got a little intimate with the bottom on his first few attempts and gave himself a mega bruise on one of his knobby knees and added a couple of hair-removing scrapes to his elbow, but all in all, he's a natural. I shouldn't be surprised, though. He's a natural magician too. In fact, he's good at all the things I like to do. If he wasn't an eight-foot-tall hairy monster with major BO, we could be long-lost twins. We certainly have more in common than me and Kyle.

After another run, Houdini recklessly goes for the invert (trying to show off, no doubt) and hand-plants nothing but air.

Like, misses the coping entirely. He bounces off the lip of the pool and belly flops onto the bottom.

Holy Snausages! I slide down to help him, and he jumps to his feet with an exaggerated bow.

I burst out laughing. "That was epic, Houdini."

He grabs the board, eager to go again, but I take it from him. "Maybe you should take a fiver and let me do a few runs."

He shakes his head and snatches the board.

"Uh . . . *no.*" My turn to yank the board from him except he keeps a tight grip on it, and it's a tug-of-war. "You can't hog all the fun, Houdini. Friends share."

Grumbling, he lets go, and I stumble onto my butt. He chortles. Fair enough.

Once I warm up with a few easy runs, I demonstrate a bunch of tricks, including inverts. Houdini copies my moves from the sidelines. When it's his turn again, I give him an overview of the invert, but I can tell he's too excited. Despite my warnings, he barrels down the side of the pool going eighty miles an hour.

"Slow down. For the love of cookies and cream, slow down!"

He flies out of the pool, arms and legs flailing like an upside-down beetle trying to right itself, and sails straight for the fence, the part that's not broken or missing slats. *SCHWOMP.* He slams into the boards sideways, a giant *X*, and flattens the fence.

I get there as fast as I can without a Sherpa to clear a path. Houdini's still as stone, and my heart drops. A muffled moan revives me, and I jump up with a cheer, but he turns to me with his finger to his lips. Meaning, *shush.* I swallow my relief. Because the moan, which happens again, isn't coming from him. It's coming from under the fence. Houdini snakes into the grass to hide, and I lift the broken boards.

Ripper!

He's got a gash across the bridge of his nose and splintered wood in his hair.

I glare at him. "What're you doing?"

"Nothing," he says, getting to his wobbly feet, clearly shaken. "I was just walking by and your rickety fence nearly killed me."

Maybe.

But I don't trust him.

Houdini, however, I trust 100 percent.

Example: when I return to my room, he's got the rabbit cage set up on top of the magic stand, ready to fulfill his end of the bargain. Teaching me how to make a rabbit disappear.

Same as I demonstrated skateboard tricks for him, he demonstrates magic tricks for me. First, he throws my cape over the cage to conceal it, and Abracadabra, Kalamazoo—or as he says, *doink, doink*—when he whips it off, Orville's gone.

Sweet.

He covers the cage again, and bing, bang, boom, Orville's back, unperturbed by his trip to the netherworld.

"Let me try, let me try." I bolt over, but Houdini plucks me off the ground before I get there and deposits me on the bed. He's not done showing off yet. I mean, demonstrating.

"Okay, but hurry."

Foot tapping impatiently, I watch as Houdini makes two rabbits—Orville and Smore—disappear at the same time, but reappear separately. Oh, he's good.

You'd assume he'd make Orville, Smore, and Marshmallow vanish simultaneously next, but he surprises by making the cage disappear. And not the rabbits.

"Whoa."

And when he makes the cage reappear, the rabbits are gone. His final trick returns the rabbits to their cage, and brings me to my feet.

"Bravo! Bravo!"

After bowing, he motions for me to join him behind the magic stand. Excitement and nerves wrestle for position in my stomach as I skid to a halt next to him. He raises the magician's cape up high so the make-believe audience can't see us, and then he does it.

He reveals the secret.

CHAPTER 27

Dry cleaning over my shoulder, I skate home.

Obviously, I haven't been paying attention, otherwise I'd know why Dad needs his tuxedo. I only hope it doesn't involve me.

The sound of fast-approaching skaters spikes my pulse, and I glance behind me. Good news, bad news—it's Ella, but Ripper's with her. His face has swelled since his run-in with my fence this morning, and he has a shiner under each eye. I act as though I don't give a rat's butt about them and keep going, but Ella catches up and skates alongside me. Now my pulse spikes for different reasons.

"Nice tux. Yours?" she says.

"Pfff 'ch'as if." *Sigh.* At least I'm still on my board.

Ripper flanks my other side. "We're heading to the park. You should come with us."

"Why? So you can cut me off again? Pass."

"Dude, you were wearing a *cape*," he says with a laugh, then quickly changes course. "But you're right, no excuse, that was low of me. Sorry, man."

I stop, dubious. "What do you want, Ripper? What's your game?"

They both spin 180 to face me.

"Nothing. Relax. I'm just big enough to admit when I'm wrong, that's all."

"It's true," Ella says. "He's always apologizing."

Ripper gives her a sarcastic smile, which she returns.

"To be fair," he continues, "I didn't think you'd go down. Dude, you were killing it before I dropped in. I thought I'd be the one to wipe out."

Is he for real?

"Anyway, your fence got even with me," he says. "I think it broke my nose."

Totally.

"C'mon, Monty," Ella says. "Thrash moved a bench by these stairs, and everyone's catching some hard-core air off their slides. You don't want to miss out."

There are a trillion reasons why this is a bad idea—Dad's waiting for his tux, Houdini's waiting for me, Watson's waiting to pee, but most of all, Ripper's absolutely, positively, 100 percent untrustworthy. None of that, however, overpowers my urge to be near Ella.

"Sure."

A twinge of guilt pricks my left ventricle for choosing her over Houdini, but he's got Watson to keep him company until I get home. And the truth is, much as I love having him as a friend, we don't get to do all the things real friends get to do. Like go out in broad daylight.

As we arrive at the park, Thrash nods in our general direction. Maybe at me. " 'S'up, brah?"

I wave, because apparently dorkdom is part of my DNA.

Ella was right, though—no skater would want to miss out

on this. Thrash positioned a bench off the stairs leading to one of the smaller parking lots, and it's the kind of bench with no armrests so you can slide or grind along the seat no problem. The end of it hangs over the first stair (in a set of ten), making a rad not-for-beginners curb. Case in point: a couple of guys don't clear the stairs and one of them tweaks his ankle and the other snaps a finger.

But I nail it. This is my language, and finally, people understand me.

We take turns directing traffic away from our makeshift skate park until we're outnumbered by agitated drivers, at which point we move on to the actual skate park per their unkind suggestions. And I'm a part of it all: fakies, front nose grabs, McTwists, *double* McTwists. It's like the old days, when we didn't move every six months.

When I had friends.

Our next stop is D'Onofrio's. That's the pizza place across the street from Glen Witch where kids hang out after school and where Thrash had his birthday party I wasn't invited to. We take a booth by the window, and Ella slides in beside me. *Me*. I can't believe it; our knees are practically touching. She smells good. Like apple shampoo.

Her sweet scent, however, is eclipsed by the aroma of sizzling pepperoni when they bring over our order. You can buy by the slice, but we're sharing a whole pie between the four of us—two pieces each—and we dig in like we haven't eaten in days.

It's the best pizza I've ever tasted, but I only get to taste it for a split second because I spot Houdini (!) staring up at me from under the table, frothy saliva dripping off his chin. I jolt back, startled, and choke on my first delicious bite, shooting a glob of cheesy salty mush out of my mouth. As if that's not mortifying enough, the glob lands with a wet thud inside Ella's baseball cap on the table. I couldn't make that shot again if I tried.

"Ew, gross," she says with a laugh and slides her cap over to me. "You owe me a new one."

"Dude," Ripper adds with a disgusted snort.

Miraculously, none of them notice the monster under the table. They're busy eyeballing me while protectively sliding their slices away from my hazardous mouth.

"Anchovies," I blurt out, trying to cover. "They must've put one on the pizza, and I'm allergic. I should . . . Go. Home." I direct that last part to Houdini, slipping him my slice as a bribe. He sucks it down but doesn't leave.

"See ya, wouldn't wanna be ya," Ripper says.

Ella gets up to let me out of the booth. "Later, skater."

Brilliant. I sabotaged myself, and now I have to leave. "Okay, well, time to . . . Go. Home," I say again so Houdini gets the point.

"Not standing for nothing," Ella says.

"Brah, split," Thrash chimes in, still guarding his pizza with his arms.

I drag myself out of the seat, and my new friends fall into conversation like I was never there. At least I have a souvenir—Ella's cap.

Once outside, I have to make sure Houdini's gone. I'm fairly certain he won't eat my friends, but still. Pretending to tie my shoe by the window, I glance over to check under the table. That's when I remember: Dad's tux!

I hung it on a tree branch by the stairs at the park and completely forgot about it until now, when it smacks me in the back of my head as it flies over, sailing in the wind. Not unmanned, mind you.

Paper thin, Houdini is plastered to it, steering that ship.

"Houdini," I yell-whisper, but the bagged suit hangs a left onto the next street. I'm about to chase after when screeching tires startle me into stumbling back.

From the parking space in front of me, a bony-faced, long-haired man in a white truck peels out, *backwards*, burning rubber. Then spins into a U-turn—revealing Animal Control on the side of his truck—and screeches around the corner. He's after Houdini!

Skating at breakneck speed, I round the corner, pursuing the truck, and narrowly avoid a collision with Pastrami Breath himself. Just when I exhale my relief, I'm yanked back. The old man has me in his clutches.

"Montague," he says, pulling me in for a triple air-kiss, as if we planned to meet up this way. His eye is doing that twitching thing again, and I pray it doesn't pop out.

"I really gotta go, Doctor Petrovic." I try not to panic as he keeps a tight grip on my arms, pinning me in place. I've lost sight of the Animal Control truck.

Clicking his tongue, he looks up and down the street. "Oh, Archibald? Archie? Why isn't he here? With you?"

"He's at D'Onofrio's. Please let me go."

The doc's demeanor flips instantly. "Unacceptable. Useless. I ask for one little favor." His whole eye orb bulges out as he releases me and storms off.

No time to gross out, I take off, speculating what "little favor" he asked that Ripper's not doing by being at D'Onofrio's instead of being with me. I already told him Ripper was being nice. Does he want us to be best friends? Forget it.

Making it home in record time, I race up the stairs and into my room. Houdini's not here, and I can't breathe. Did Animal Control catch up to him? I throw Ella's hat on the bed and drop to my knees to check underneath. "Houdini?"

Not there.

"Houdini?"

He doesn't emerge and I'm frantic now. Why'd I leave him behind for my own selfish desires? He needs me. He depends on me. I'm supposed to be there for him. I promised; I promised he could count on me.

Near tears, I empty the magic stand (throwing items over my head behind me), dig through the pillowcase until it rains feathers, and scour the closet—all his old haunts—but they're monster-free.

"Houdini?"

"Who's Houdini?" Dad says.

Agh!

He's in the doorway.

I stifle my tears and force a laugh. "Who's Houdini? Only the greatest escape artist ever. I was channeling his essence." Oh, brother. That's lame even for me.

He buys it, though, and enters with a smile. "A master, indeed."

"Well, I should get back to it." I try to usher him out, but he's planted.

"Kyle said you offered to pick up my tux. Thanks."

"What are kids for?" I try to encourage him out again with a guiding hand.

"Where'd you put it? It's not in my room."

"Oh. Right. Put it. Where . . . did . . . I . . . put it?" I speak slowly, trying to come up with a plan as I check under the bed, in the closet, behind the curtains. "Tuxedo. Tuxedo."

SLAM!

Dad and I share a heart attack, but hanging on the back of my bedroom door, settling in, is the tuxedo.

"There. It's right there."

"Thanks again, Monty. I appreciate you helping out."

He takes the bagged suit and throws it over his shoulder. On the backside, Houdini looks at me with drooping eyes and yawns as Dad unwittingly carries him away. I'm drenched in relief.

Old doors creak.

And Dad's is no exception. He stirs, snoring interrupted. I freeze, the door halfway open, and brace myself. Two seconds later, he snores again, and I enter.

He's sleeping in his chair. The recliner, except it's not reclined. He was watching home movies. The ones of him and Mom, before us. I know because he's got the old camcorder hooked up to his TV. Kyle's always on him to transfer the tapes before they disintegrate, but I think Dad subconsciously wants to let them fade. As if once the images disappear, so will his sadness. I know he'll feel worse not having them, but sometimes grown-ups do stupid things too.

With the tux nowhere in sight, it doesn't take a detective to deduce it's probably in the closet, which is on the other side of the chair Dad's occupying. That's the way my day's been going—nothing's easy.

Tiptoeing across the squeaky floors, I plan to tell him I heard a noise and was scared if he wakes up. He likes it when I need him, whether it's a homework question, a scraped knee, or a random hug. The latter has sort of disappeared lately.

I make it to the closet undetected and quietly twist the knob and open the door. The tux is still in the plastic wrapping adorned by Houdini on one side who, like Dad, is sound asleep and snoring.

Finger to my lips, I tap his shoulder gently. Houdini pops open his eyes with a start but warms immediately upon seeing me. He peels himself from the bag, and we sneak out. I hope Dad's dreaming good dreams about Mom.

CHAPTER 28

N o can do, Houdini."

My tone is firm, but I'm laughing tears on the inside. Houdini's stuffed into my clothes, backpack over his shoulder. He thinks he can go to school with me dressed as a boy. On him, my jeans reach his knobby knees (and only because he has short legs for an eight-foot-tall monster), and my T-shirt barely covers his chest.

Doink, doink. That means *please*. I'm an expert at interpreting his expressive blinks.

"School is for people, not monsters pretending to be people."

Doink—

"No," I interrupt. "We've been through this. You're not people."

He points to his two arms then to mine, to his two legs then to mine, eyes, nose, mouth, and ears and then to mine.

"Lots of living things have all the same components, Houdini. It doesn't make them the same. Besides, my friends won't understand."

He takes the *F* word hard, and his lip trembles.

"Well, you didn't expect me to never have friends, did you?"
He points to himself.

"I mean real friends." Houdini dives into the magic stand, and I hear the trapdoor slam shut underneath. "I meant *people* friends," I say quietly, mostly to appease myself.

Now Watson gives me a disapproving look. I can't win. Grabbing my backpack and board, I head out.

Ella exits her house the same time as me, also carrying her board, and embarrassment washes over me, but I remind myself she doesn't know (and never will) that I sleep with her baseball cap under my pillow. Spot-washing it got the food out while leaving the apple-shampoo scent on the rest of it.

I wave, ready to pull the old fix-my-hair move, but she waves back.

"Hi, Monty."

"Hi-llo." *Srsly.*

She snorts adorably. "You're funny."

Score. She thinks I did it on purpose. We walk, even though we have our boards.

"So, Spanish Club," I say.

"Is that a question?"

"Uh. No. I mean, yeah. I was thinking of joining."

"Is *that* a question?"

"No. Well, sort of. I was wondering if you thought it was a good idea."

"How would I know?"

"Aren't you in it?"

"Because I'm Latina? Kinda presumptuous of you, isn't it?"
My cheeks are on fire.

"Psych! Of course I am," she says. "You should come. We don't have any guys in there."

"Not even Ripper?"

"Ripper? He barely gets through his classes. He's not gonna do an extracurricular activity."

"Oh, I just thought, you know, since he's your boyfriend."

"Ew." She shoves me. "Why would you think that?"

"Because you're always together."

"Yeah, it's called being friends. I've known him since kindergarten."

"Really? Was he a jerk back then too?"

"You mean *jackass?*" she says, amused, and I remember she was there for our fight after school. She probably thinks I started it.

"I was retaliating."

"How'd that go?"

Smart aleck. "I had to. He's been bullying me since I got here."

"I get it. You gotta stand up for yourself."

"Exactly. You saw him cut me off at the skate park."

"You looked like one of those chalk outlines." She cracks up, and imitates me by bending her arms and legs in contorted directions.

Oh, good. I get to relive the embarrassment.

When she stops laughing at my expense, she says, "It was low of him, for sure, but he's actually a nice guy deep down, believe it or not."

Not.

"And just so you know, we all rag on each other's wipeouts, so if we're gonna hang out together, you can't take it personally."

Hold everything. Did she flat-out confirm our friendship?

No more pining. Spying. Anticipating. I'm on cloud nine. Not even Ripper, who ollies onto the sidewalk to join us, can ruin my mood.

"I see the anchovies didn't kill ya," he says.

"Yeah. That was a close one."

As if we'd been doing this all along, we skate to school together, picking up Thrash along the way. Lunch is a whole new experience when friends are part of the equation. For one thing, you get to eat your food instead of cleaning it up off the floor. And after PE, I don't have to put my jeans on over my gym shorts and run for my life. Best of all, by the time school's out, I'm no longer exhausted, I'm exhilarated.

Ripper catches up to me as I exit Glen Witch. Full confession: I meandered out of the building slower than a sloth, wishing Ella would emerge.

"Everyone's meeting at the skate park," he says. "But I locked myself outta the house and don't have my pads. You got an extra set?"

Everyone has to include Ella. "Sure."

We skate on the sidewalk, doing some tricks. Nothing too serious.

"So does your dad work at the university too?" I ask.

"Not anymore. He's dead. So's my mom."

Stunned, I inadvertently shoot the board away from me in the middle of my 180 No Comply. It doesn't get far, and I grab it. "Dead? They're both dead?"

"Yeah. It happens, you know."

"I know. It's just . . . that sucks."

"Well, that's life for ya. Everything's great one second and horrible the next."

He's trying to play if off like it's nothing, but I'm overcome with compassion. Losing my mom was the worst thing ever. Both parents? I can't even.

"Don't get all weird," he says off my silence. "It's been over a year. I'm used to it now."

He isn't, but I finally understand why Ella gives him a pass.

"So you live with Doctor Petrovic, then? I mean, your grandfather?"

"Sort of. He works a lot so I mostly live alone if you think about it. It's pretty stellar, actually. I got the run of the house. Watch whatever I want whenever I want. Eat whatever I want. No one to get on me to do my homework or get good grades. I'm living the dream."

"Yeah." His dream made me sad.

"Righteous room, dude."

Unbelievable! Ripper, who I distinctly told to stay downstairs, is in my room, and I'm torso-deep into one of the huge cardboard packing boxes, digging for my extra pads. I flail my way out in a hurry. I've got a monster sulking somewhere in here; I can't have people snooping around.

"I told you to wait downstairs, Ripper."

"Your dog brought me up." Watson stands by his side, not the least bit remorseful. Ripper surveys the room, hatching a storm of butterflies in my stomach. I have one thing to hide but feel like I have a million.

"Got the pads. Let's go." I hasten for the door, but Ripper breezes over to the magic stand.

"What's this?" He sticks his face inside before I can stop him, and I cringe, bracing for Houdini to pop up thinking it's me. He doesn't.

"A magic stand. Let's go."

"Dude, there's a trapdoor under here."

"No, there's not."

"Yeah. Look." He pushes the stand aside and opens the

trapdoor. Again, I cringe, but Houdini doesn't emerge. "Where does it go?"

"To China. Where do you think?"

"Why're you being all cagey? What's down there?"

"Nothing interesting. Just a dark, moldy cellar."

"Excellent." He hops in and takes the rope ladder like an athlete. No choice, I follow.

"It's a bunch of old junk. It's not like there's anything to *hide*," I say loudly so Houdini will take the hint if he's down here.

The grate lowers us into the cellar where the bare bulb sways ever so slightly over the lab table. I take that to mean Houdini was here.

Like a moth, Ripper gravitates toward the light and sizes everything up with a cursory glance. "This is my grandfather's stuff."

Is not! Finders keepers. "No. It was here when we moved in," I say.

"Yeah, 'cause someone dumped it here, obviously. It's all my grandfather talks about. How Dean Smith shut down his research way back when and confiscated everything. He's been looking for this for decades."

Ripper picks up a beaker and sniffs it, then moves on to a petri dish. I hate that he's rummaging through my lab, but I let him. It gives me more time to scan the cellar for signs of Houdini. Either he's hiding (good), or he left (even better).

"Dude." Ripper snaps his fingers in my face, pulling my attention back to him.

"Huh? What?"

"What're you looking for?"

"Nothing!" I say way too emphatically.

"Yeah, that's not suspicious." He motions to the crates. "You know this stuff is toxic, right? Like three-eyes-five-arms real-life-mutant toxic."

"All right, then, let's get outta here."

He folds his arms and coolly leans back against the table. "Why?"

"What do you mean *why*? You just said why. Toxic. Mutants."

"But you already know that."

My face drains of blood. *Is he saying what I think he's saying?*

"I saw it, Monty. The butt-ugly hairy giant."

Holy crap, he is. Run! No wait. Calm down, stop trembling, play dumb. "No idea what you're talking about."

"You made it out of my grandfather's stuff, didn't you? Where is it?"

My throat is a desert all of a sudden, and I'm unable to speak.

"Really? You're gonna be like that?"

"Like what?" I manage to squeak out.

"I saw it," he says again, as if hearing it a second time will make me confess.

I shrug, feigning ignorance. "Sorry. You lost me."

Ripper snorts. "Should've known. Poser, through and through." He pivots and marches off.

Unexpectedly, his words sting, but I can't argue. I'm not a real friend. My motives are Ella-driven, period.

I wait until he disappears up the grate, then scour the cellar for Houdini. What a disaster. Not only do I have to explain the gravity of this to Houdini, I've gotta figure out how to convince Ripper he didn't see what he clearly saw.

"Houdini?" I shout-whisper. "Stop acting like a baby and come out."

A shrill scream bounces off the interior walls of the passageway, then stops abruptly. The floor becomes ice as I skitter to get there, begging *please please please*. I'm not exactly sure what I'm begging for but something like *please don't have eaten the most popular kid at Glen Witch*.

Houdini leaps down from the passageway before I cover any ground. Teeth bared, he's clutching a very alive Ripper under his arm with his hand over Ripper's mouth.

Ripper trembles and a stream of sweat drips off his temple.

"Houdini, I said no more people burgers."

Houdini drops Ripper to the floor, shaking his head to let me know I misunderstand. Ripper scrambles back on all fours, but Houdini stomps down on his ankle, pinning him in place. Ripper yelps.

"Let him go. I mean it."

Grumbling, Houdini lifts his foot, and Ripper dodges behind me for cover. "Keep that thing away from me."

"We had a deal," I tell Houdini. "No eating people or pets, and you stay hidden. What gives?"

Houdini points to Ripper.

"I told you, I have other friends now. You're going to have to get used to it."

Houdini narrows his eyes and shakes his head no.

"He's not mean to me anymore."

DOINK, he shouts and reaches for Ripper, but I latch onto his hairy finger, stopping him.

"We don't hurt people, Houdini. No ifs, ands, or buts."

He slouches with sad blinks, and I release my grip on his finger. He keeps his head bowed, scolded.

"It's even uglier up close," Ripper says as he eases out from behind me.

"*He*, not it. And he's not ugly. Not once you get to know

him. He's exactly as he should be."

"Rank?"

"I'll give you that one."

Houdini rolls his eyes, sick of hearing it.

"When did you see him?" I ask Ripper.

"When your fence creamed me, genius. You were out in the open."

"I was in my backyard. Private property."

"It's not my fault your fence is more holes than fence."

He's right. It might as well be chain link for all it masks. At least I know Houdini wasn't spotted at school or D'Onofrio's or anywhere else around town. In fact, it's troubling he got sloppy now when he's an expert at staying hidden. Maybe jealousy got the better of him.

"Does your dad know?" Ripper asks.

"No one does. And if you rat me out, I swear—"

"Dude. We're friends," Ripper says with a reassuring smile. "I got your back."

Now I smile. Maybe we are. For real.

Houdini pouts.

CHAPTER 29

Where does he poop?

Why does he smell? Does he really eat people? Can I grow one out of my shoe? How old is he? Does Watson like him?

Ripper won't shut up now that he knows about Houdini. I had to physically drag him out of the house so we could hit the park as planned. Never mind how impossible it was to squeeze a promise out of Houdini to stay put.

On a normal day, we'd be there in minutes, but Ripper's skating way too leisurely for my anxiety level (he's more interested in asking a bazillion questions), and I'm about to explode. I need to get to the bowl and burn off some angst. After working so hard to keep Houdini under wraps, poof, gone in an instant. The rest of my life will be on pins and needles, waiting for Ripper to slip up. I just hope the others don't ask what took us so long to get there.

"Why are you keeping him a secret, anyway?" Ripper asks. "You could be famous. People would come from all over the world to see him."

"That's exactly why. I don't want anyone taking advantage of him. He's got feelings, you know."

"What about Ella? Aren't you gonna tell her? I know you're crushing on her."

"What? Crushing? No. Where'd you get—no. As if. Crushing."

"Bummer. She told me she likes you."

"She did? What did she say? What were her exact words?"

"Something like you're cute in a dorky way."

That totally sounds like her. "No way! What else?"

Ripper bursts into laughter, unable to hold a straight face. "Sorry, man. I couldn't resist. Too easy."

Jerk. I skate ahead, but he catches up to me.

"C'mon, dude. It was a joke."

"Whatever. I don't even like her."

"It's not a crime to like someone, Monty. Relax."

Easy for you to say. You're popular.

We skate the rest of the way one-upping each other with tricks until I'm no longer mad at him and we're laughing at our wipeouts.

When we arrive at the skate park, Ella and Thrash hurry over to greet us, but Ripper pulls Thrash with him toward the bowl, leaving me alone with Ella. It's his way of making up for teasing me, but Ella doesn't know that.

"Hi to you too," she says to the back of his head. She turns to me. "What took you guys so long?"

"Diarrhea." *Crickets!* I've got to stop blurting out the first thing that comes to mind.

"What?" She chuckle-snorts, and I instantly flash back to the day Houdini hitched a ride to school with me and she passed by the stench. She must think I have serious stomach issues.

"Not me. Watson. I don't have diarrhea. I mean, not that

I've never had it. That would be a lie. Everyone gets diarrhea, even you." *Stop talking.* "Anyway, super messy. Not yours. I'm sure yours was fine. Well, I wouldn't know." *Why am I still talking?* "Watson's. Watson's was a mess. I had to clean it up. That's what took so long. Cleaning up Watson's diarrhea."

She stares at me with the same expression I had when I first saw our house. Then she cracks a smile and shoves me. "You're so funny. Come on." She heads to the snake run, and I tag alongside.

If there was such a thing as a perfect day, this would be it. But there isn't. There's always something to ruin perfection. Today, it's the Animal Control truck parked on the path behind the Science building, on the other side of the park. That skinny, long-haired man leans against the driver's side door, watching. Me, I think.

He knows I'm not an animal, doesn't he? My stomach sinks with the revelation that maybe he has seen Houdini on one of his jaunts and maybe he was after him that day at D'Onofrio's and maybe Houdini's here now.

"I gotta go," I say to Ella, and she actually looks disappointed.

"You just got here."

"Yeah, I lied. I'm the one with diarrhea." I had to. It's a conversation ender.

"Okay. Later, skater," she says, grossed out. I assume, because who wouldn't be? She changes course to meet up with Ripper and Thrash without a glance back. I turn to leave and— *eep!*— the guy is leaning on the gates to the skate park.

Definitely watching me.

He's got on white pants and a white button-down shirt with the name tag sewn above the pocket. Animal Control: Schmelding. Up close, he looks like a skeleton. Dark circles under his sunken eyes, bony cheeks, no lips to speak of. He winks.

I run, skateboard under my arm, past the tennis courts, through the basketball court, across the soccer field, until I reach the pathway and hop on my board. If Houdini did sneak out of the house (when he totally shouldn't have!), I certainly hope he grasps the dire situation and gets home, undetected.

CHAPTER 30

Aggggggh!"

That's not me screaming. It's coming from the kitchen. I've barely got the front door open, and Watson is scurrying over so fast he crashes into me before I'm inside. He's not greeting me, though; he's crying for help and scrambles back toward the kitchen. I'm right behind him and burst in, reflexes on high alert.

Yeow-za! Houdini's got Kyle's entire leg in his mouth as Kyle pushes against his face with his other leg, trying to free himself. Dad has Houdini in a choke hold, but Houdini is upright so Dad's hanging on, feet off the ground. In spite of all this, I'm actually relieved he's home, safe and sound, and not with that Animal Control whacko.

"Houdini, are you trying to get us in trouble?"

Houdini brightens at the sight of me and sticks out his tongue to show me he's not eating Kyle; he's got his tongue wrapped around his leg (like a taco shell) to keep him at bay. It's two against one, after all. Obs he was in one of his food comas when they took him by surprise—there are food wrappings abound, and my backpack is overstuffed with snacks.

"Call 9-1-1. Call 9-1-1!" Dad yells.

As if. "Let him go, Houdini."

Houdini unfolds his tongue, and Kyle drops to the floor and skitters over to me. Dad releases his choke hold and grabs the broom, jumping between Houdini and us.

"Stay back," he says, jabbing the air with his flimsy weapon.

"Calm down, Dad. This is Houdini. The monster I told you about."

Houdini blinks *hello*, but an eight-foot-tall creature with razor-sharp teeth and long claws is frightening any which way if you don't personally know him.

Dad keeps his weapon trained. "Are you telling me this thing has been in our house the whole time? What were you thinking, Monty? You put us all in danger. You can't keep this. Do you even know what it is? It needs to be examined and identified and catalogued for crying out loud. It's a monster!"

"I know. That's what I've been saying. But he's harmless."

Houdini, the master of poor timing, burps—wet, loud, and smelly.

"Ugh." Kyle grabs his stomach. "Now we know what happened to your babysitter."

"What?" Dad says, devastated. "This thing ate Becky?"

"No," I jump in before panic escalates into bedlam. "He doesn't eat people." *Anymore.* "That's liver breath. I have to feed him so I made meat brownies."

"It almost ate your brother; don't tell me it doesn't eat people. Get my phone."

"No. You can't take him from me. He's my friend. I made him."

"Not up for negotiation."

"That's not fair. You always say that when you want to get your way."

"Montague Hyde, you do as I say or you're grounded for life."

"No."

"Monty—"

"No!"

Dad clenches his jaw. I've never seen him this irate. "You're grounded. Kyle, bring me my phone."

"Monty!"

I tear out of the house on my skateboard with my backpack hanging off my shoulder, Houdini tucked inside it. Both Dad and Watson chase after me, but only Watson catches up. Kyle could've easily beaten me to the door, but he was upstairs getting Dad's phone.

"Montague Hyde, you get back here," Dad yells, but I keep going. Watson runs alongside me.

Houdini pops his head out of my backpack, creating drag, and without stopping, I stuff him back in. Five blocks deeper into Crampus, I realize I should've skated the other way, out of the gates. Fact is, I didn't give this any thought at all. Flee first, ask questions later. Except don't ask questions you already know the answer to.

Dad's a scientist, and when a scientist takes something to the lab, it's not good for the something. Well, Houdini's not some *thing*. He's a living, breathing creature. He has feelings. And I can't let Dad experiment on him.

Unfortunately, I dumped the snacks from my backpack to make room for Houdini, and I can already hear his stomach complaining. It's getting dark, which is good for hiding, but what happens when hunger brings out the monster in him? There's only one person I can turn to; one person who knows my secret.

A block from Ripper's house, I hop off my board and walk lightly so his grandfather won't hear me if he's home. Their house isn't ramshackle like mine, but up close, there are signs of neglect. Chipped paint, gutters overflowing with leaves, a loose railing, cracked steps to their porch.

Lights are on inside.

I duck into the bushes on the side of the house and peer through one of the windows. I can see the living room and probably what would be the dining room, but you'd never know it because the house is practically empty. There's a recliner in the living room, a folding tray and folding chair in the dining room, both unfolded and ready for use, and a floor lamp. That's it. Ripper said he was living the life. I envisaged him having all the cool stuff I longed for.

Dr. Petrovic appears from out of nowhere in front of the window I'm staring through. Maybe it's his twitching eye or because it's nighttime, but he doesn't see me. I drop to my belly, and the light coming from inside disappears. The old doc closed the curtains.

I still don't know if Ripper's home, and I can't call him because I don't have my phone. Flat on the ground, I remind Watson to be quiet with a finger to my lip, and slither farther into the side yard. Two very familiar, very hairy legs in a pair of Vans sneakers block my path. I jump up. Houdini has a petrified Ripper under his arm with a hand over Ripper's mouth.

"Houdini!" I whisper while checking my backpack as if that has the answer as to how he snuck out without me noticing. I should try to remember he can't stay small forever.

Smiling proudly, he blinks. *Doink, doink.*

"Yes, I was looking for him, but you can't just go and take people. Especially without asking me first."

Houdini about-faces to return Ripper to the house, but I grab his arm to stop him. "Well, now that you've got him . . ." I motion for him to let Ripper down.

"Still stinks," Ripper says as he takes a few steps back. "What're you doing here?"

"Running away."

"To here?"

"No. But I don't know where to go with a giant monster I'm trying to keep hidden. My dad saw Houdini and wants to take him to the lab. You know what that means."

Ripper lights up. "Dude, that's exactly where you should go."

"Are you nuts? They'll cut him open and rip out his guts."

Houdini shrieks and quickly covers his own mouth to silence himself. I take his hand to reassure him. "Don't worry, Houdini. I won't let anyone hurt you."

"No one's getting sliced and diced, 'cause no one would think to look for you there," Ripper says. "It'd just be for the night. I can sneak you in, run out and get some pizzas, and we can figure out our next move."

"Really? You'd do that for us?"

"Of course. We're friends, aren't we?"

Houdini points from himself to Ripper back to himself.

"Yeah," Ripper says. "All of us."

I fight my stupid emotions, pushing aside the lump in my throat. "Thanks."

"No sweat."

CHAPTER 31

The doors to the Science building are locked.

Inside, at the information desk, a security guard unwraps a meatball sub, pressing the paper flat with care.

"Maybe this isn't such a good idea," I whisper. "He'd have to be blind not to see us."

"Trust me," Ripper says, with all the confidence in the world.

I sink into the wall, out of view from the doors, and motion for Houdini to do the same. He's carrying Watson—his suggestion—and I have to admit it's a good one. Ripper rings the bell, and a moment later, the guard undoes the chains on the inside and opens the door.

"No one's here, kid. Not even your grandfather."

"Doi. He asked me to get his pleura plexus arthropod incubator," Ripper says earnestly.

I bite my lips together to suppress laughter.

"All right, make it quick," the guard says, and Ripper enters.

His plan is to engage the guard in conversation, making him turn his back to the door, so we can sneak in.

"Hey, I don't suppose you want to go down there and get it for me?" Ripper says.

I take a peek. Unless the guard has eyes in the back of his head, we're good to go. We tiptoe in and head for the stairs while Ripper keeps him distracted.

"You just have to be careful not to touch the larvae or they'll burrow into your skin and crawl to your brain. Then one day, when you think you have a splitting headache—WHAM!— your head explodes, and tiny little eggs fly all over the place and hatch so that they can find other people to use as nesting grounds."

Houdini hijacks the meatball sub as we pass the desk, but it's too risky to do anything about it now. I pull him into the stairwell, and soon as I do, I hear Ripper say, "Never mind."

I race down to the basement and through the corridor to rejoin Ripper by the other stairwell. From there, we all sprint, except Watson, who is still being transported by Houdini. The door to Dr. Petrovic's lab is locked, but Ripper has a key. Perks to being the grandkid.

"We have all night to figure out our next move," Ripper says. "You can relax. You're safe here."

Houdini deposits Watson on the floor (to Watson's relief), and pulls Ripper in for a hug.

"What's happening?" Ripper says, muffled.

"He's thanking you."

I await the tough guy to push him away, but he doesn't. A few moments later, he asks, "How long does it last?"

"Long as you let it."

He lets it for another few moments then slips free. "So, pizza, right?"

Houdini gives a hardy thumbs-up.

"As many as you can," I say.

"You got it. Back in twenty."

On his way out, Ripper hesitates by the door, then turns to me. My heart seizes. He's having second thoughts. He's bailing on me. I'm doomed.

"Pepperoni?" he says.

I exhale. "Perfect."

He exits, leaving me alone in the creepy lab (if you don't count my basset and my monster). Last time I was here, a corpse lay on a table. It's gone, but the CryogenOrgans freezer isn't. It's staring at me, inviting me to look inside.

"You guys stay here," I tell Houdini and Watson. I ease toward it, keeping an eye out for zombies hiding in the shadows, and notice something wedged partway behind a cabinet against the wall.

It's one of those compact videotapes similar to the kind Dad used to record on when he used to be happy. It's jammed in there good, but my fingers are small enough to wriggle it loose. The case is scratched up and dusty, but I can read the label on the tape. *05.05.1989 Final Test.*

May fifth, nineteen eighty-nine. That syncs up with the *Human Replication and Reanimation* journal. I bet Dr. Petrovic recorded his experiments.

Eager to check it out, I search for a tape player or TV combo-type thing, but don't find one. I slip the tape in my pocket for later, and turn my attention back to the macabre freezer. Before I do anything, I put on protective goggles and canvas gloves (like the ones Dad wore when he handled that heart). Prepped, I unlatch the door. A cloud of wispy smoke, like dry ice, wafts out, blocking my view, but it dissipates soon enough.

"Whoa."

Hearts. Brains. Livers. Spongy-looking stuff.

Real-life organs stuffed into jars, dozens of them. A week

ago, innards grossed me out. Now, I imagine all the friends I can make with these parts.

Tsh. Tsh.

Houdini's slobber splashes my feet as he ogles the organs. So much for staying put when I tell him to. Watson's no better, wagging his tail alongside his new bestie.

"Sorry, Houdini, that's not for eating."

He whimpers.

"I know, but Ripper will be back soon with pizza. Remember pizza? You liked it."

In fact, I can smell the pepperoni now. Has it been twenty minutes already?

I turn to greet Ripper and instead find the wild-eyed Dr. Petrovic between us and the exit, holding a dozen steaming pizza boxes. Next to him, the Animal Control guy, Schmelding, cradles a catch pole in one hand and a Taser in the other.

# CHAPTER 32

Backstabbing, two-faced phony!

That duplicitous sack of dung sold us out to his crazy organ-harvesting grandfather.

Houdini tries to make a dash for the pizzas, but I block his path with my arm, and he reads my fury well enough to stop. Watson growls but doesn't attack. That's pretty much his MO, and I appreciate the effort, but sometimes, you need an attack dog.

"Thank you, Montague, for returning what is rightfully mine," Dr. Petrovic says, eyeballing Houdini. As if Houdini is his!

I remove the goggles and gloves. "Get out of the way."

"You're free to go anytime you want. But the magnificent giant stays."

"Over my dead body."

"Is that an offer? Because I have a form."

He does. He produces a form. Maybe if I agree to sign it, he'll approach, leaving enough room for us to get past the armed Schmelding. That freak's grinning, like he wants to hurt us.

"Do you have any idea where your monster came from?" the doctor asks.

Der. "I made him."

He laughs. And holds up the vial of incandescent green slime. *My* green slime!

It hits me like a sucker punch to the gut.

Ripper didn't merely rat me out; he set me up from the start.

He never wanted to be my friend. It was all pretense so he could snoop around my house for his twisted grandfather. The one little favor. And Houdini tried to warn me. He must've seen Ripper steal the vial, but I wouldn't listen.

"That's mine!" I reach for it, but Schmelding zaps the air with his Taser, keeping me at bay.

"It's mine," Dr. Petrovic says, his pesky eye twitching and bulging. "Everything in that cellar is mine." He approaches, and each step he takes forward, Houdini, Watson, and I step back. "I was this-close to discovering the key to immortality when they confiscated my research. All of it, gone!" He breaks into a smile, and one of his teeth falls out. "But now I have everything I need." He doesn't even pick up his tooth. "You see, never did my formula create life from nothing. This creature is the missing link. And when I reveal it at the fundraiser, the dean will open the coffers to the science department." He pauses for effect it seems, then shouts, "*Now*, Schmelding!"

Huh? What?

Schmelding yanks a lever on other side of the room, and an earsplitting *CAGUNK* floors my heart rate. Before I can register what's happening, a metal cage drops from the ceiling, slamming into the floor, missing me by inches. Watson yelps, also in the clear, but it's got Houdini. That devious doctor backed him into a trap.

"Ta-ta, toodles," he says to me. "Move along."

Instinct takes over, and I kick him in the shin and snatch the vial of green slime from him. "C'mon, Houdini!"

I bolt for the door as Dr. Petrovic reels on the ground, cradling his pained leg, and Schmelding dive-rolls to his aid, crying, "Why? Why!"

Watson skitters on the vinyl tiles and can't get going, but Houdini squeezes through the bars of the cage, like I knew he could, and hefts Watson into his arms (while devouring two whole pizzas) as we flee the lab at warp speed.

Behind us, Petrovic yells at Schmelding to leave him alone and go after us. We tear into the stairwell and race up to the first floor. *Fudge nuts!* I see it before I reach them. The doors to the outside are locked. Chains on. I about-face, and run down the corridor. "This way."

There's gotta be another exit. Rounding the corner, I slam into the security guard and bounce off his barrel chest, stunned. I land on my butt next to Watson, who's splayed out on his belly like Superman flying. That's because the master of escape is gone. Disappeared. Uplifted that he made a break for it, I have to get Watson and myself out now. I need to come up with something, and quick.

"What're you doing here? How'd you get in?" the security guard demands to know.

"Who, me?" Turns out, I'm not that quick.

"Yeah, you. Unless your dog can talk."

I laugh, stalling, since my brain isn't giving me anything to work with. "That's a good one. Talking dog. No, I don't think my dog can talk. Well, I don't know, I never asked. Watson, can—"

"You got two seconds, kid, or I'm reporting you for breaking and entering."

Kyle will never cover for me if I get hauled in again. "I came here with Doctor Petrovic."

"Nice try, but I let him in tonight, and only his assistant was with him."

"I mean, this morning. He's been helping me with my science fair project. I've been here all day."

Schmelding skips into the corridor with a teeth-baring grin. "There you are," he says to me. "We mustn't keep Dr. Petrovic waiting."

"Uh, actually, I'm all set," I say to Schmelding. "That's why I was heading home."

Schmelding puts a firm hand on my shoulder, squeezing hard enough to shoot pain down my leg and stop me from moving. "Not quite. The doctor has a few more instructions for you."

Satisfied, the security guard nods. "Well, good luck with the fair, kid."

He strolls down the hall, and I swallow a gasp, not believing my eyes. Houdini's fingers are wrapped around the guard's boot from beneath, like a wrap-around spider. That's where he disappeared to. He's smooshed on the sole of the boot, hitching a ride.

Schmelding doesn't notice, but Watson and I share a glance. When the guard goes into the men's room (unwittingly taking Houdini with him), Schmelding snarls at me.

"Where's the ugly one?" he says.

"I'm looking at him."

He squeezes harder, and I buckle to one knee. "Ow!"

"We can start with the dog if you prefer."

I sink my teeth into Schmelding's stringy thigh, and he

yelps, releasing his grip. No one threatens Watson! Shuffling to my feet, I bolt in the opposite direction of the bathroom, giving Houdini more freedom to escape with Schmelding chasing me.

I dart into the stairwell and go up. Poor Watson hasn't seen this much exercise in . . . ever. By the time Schmelding yanks open the door on the first floor, I'm silently closing the one on the second floor. Like I hoped, he descends.

I've been in enough schools to know the bathrooms are stacked, meaning they're in the same place on every floor. That in mind, I find the men's room on this floor, then take the stairs closest to it back down to the first floor. Peeking out, I catch the security guard walking down the hall, but I'm too far away to see if Houdini's still on his shoe. Ideally, Houdini has squeezed out a window or vent, but I have to check. I can't abandon him and hope for the best. When the guard disappears around the corner, I sneak into the bathroom.

BAM! Before I can scope out the place, the door flies open behind me as Dr. Petrovic sails past—in midair—and hits the floor, sliding on his belly as he scans under every stall. I drop to my hands and knees, looking for Houdini's feet, but all the stalls are empty. A small window high up on the wall is open, and I'm certain Houdini made his escape.

"Drat!" Dr. Petrovic curses, brushing himself off. He leans into me, spitting mad, saliva shooting through the gap where his tooth used to be. "Where is he?"

"I don't know. I just had to pee."

Up close, his yellow skin has a waxy appearance. His crazy eye twitches—that's a given—but his good eye joins in sporadically. Finally, the madman straightens up, and his eyes normalize.

Glad to be rid of his pastrami breath, I relax. And that's when I see it. A few strands of hair sticking out from the gap in one of the stalls. Houdini *is* here. He must be wallpapered on the back of the door. Another hair unfurls, popping out, and then another. His hiding feats take a great amount of effort, and he's exhausted. Another hair and another. He's losing it; he can't hold on much longer. I need to get Petrovic out of here stat.

"You'll never catch him, not even with your scooter," I say. It's called reverse psychology. "I'm sure he's halfway home by now."

It works. The doctor pivots for the exit.

I'm about to follow when a tuft of fur floats through the air, wafting, feather-like, toward the floor. Like a bad dream, I watch, paralyzed. *No, no, no.*

But the tuft lands with an unspoken *poof,* and I'm in the clear. *Phew.* I smile.

Dr. Petrovic, however, spins. He actually heard that. He zeroes in on the tuft with an evil grin and marches to the stall, slamming it open so hard Houdini falls off.

"Run, Houdini!"

Schmelding appears in the bathroom doorway, snagging Watson with his catch pole, and zaps the Taser as a warning.

"Go ahead. Run," Dr. Petrovic says. "And the boy and his dog stay."

Houdini turns to me, worried. And sad. I've never seen him this way. He looks smaller, skinnier, weaker.

"I'll be fine, Houdini, I promise. Just run," I plead. "Run!"

But he doesn't. Because he's my friend. My real friend. And he won't let anything happen to me. Tears stream down my face.

CHAPTER 33

My bedroom is a lifeless void.

Even when Houdini was hiding, I felt his presence. Watson tries to console me, but he's sad too. His head rests on my thigh, and every once in a while, a quiet moan comes from him. The twin bed feels too big without my giant friend.

I'd scream some more, but my throat is raw from having it out with Dad for the better part of the night. After I told him everything that happened, explained how we were captured, escaped, chased, and nearly zapped, after telling him about the eye and tooth and begging him to take me back there so I could get Houdini and bring him home where he belongs, Dad had the gall—the despicable, merciless gall—to side with Dr. Petrovic. He said I was lucky the doctor wasn't pressing charges for breaking into his lab. As if Houdini's life means nothing. Said I should be thankful I wouldn't be punished for running away. Clueless to why I ran in the first place.

I hate myself for thinking I could count on him. He doesn't care about anyone but himself these days. *Give him a break, Kyle says. He's trying to adjust.* Well, who isn't? He's not the only one who lost Mom. He's not the only one suffering.

Darn it. Crying again, I wipe my face. My head already pounds from all the sobbing. I hear Dad scaling the rope ladder inside the secret passageway, returning from the cellar, and my tears dry up real quick. Carefully but quickly I tuck the vial of slime inside Ella's cap underneath my pillow. Dr. Petrovic was so overjoyed when he snagged Houdini, he forgot about the vial.

"Why didn't you tell me about those crates before?" Dad says as he emerges. He's got Dr. Petrovic's journal, and I curse myself for not thinking to hide it.

"Why would I? I told you a lot of things, but you didn't believe me 'cause all you care about is work."

"That's not true, Monty." He sits on the bed and tries to cradle my cheek in his hand, but I squirm out of it. He doesn't take the hint. "I care about you and Kyle more than anything in this world. I know it's unfair to expect you to understand, but that's why I'm working so hard right now. I promise it won't be forever."

More promises. My jaw hurts from clenching.

"Doctor Petrovic said you have his serum. A green serum. Where is it? I didn't see any down there."

"It's gone. What does it matter? Why won't you help Houdini?"

"Baby—"

"I'm not a baby."

"Monty, we don't know what that creature is."

"He's my friend."

"He ate the neighborhood students."

"He was hungry. You wouldn't get mad at a lion for eating, would you?"

"That's exactly my point. You wouldn't want a lion loose in the neighborhood, would you?"

"Not fair. You're twisting my example. He was just surviving, but he doesn't need to hunt anymore. I feed him."

"Monty, we don't know what he's capable of. He could be dangerous. At the very least, unpredictable. Please try to understand, I need to keep you safe."

"He won't hurt me. He won't hurt anyone. I'm telling you. He knows not to hurt people. Or pets. Ask Watson."

"I'm sorry. This is nonnegotiable. We need to keep him confined until we can learn more about him."

"He doesn't belong in a cage. He has feelings. What's wrong with you? Don't you have a heart?" I'm openly crying, but I don't care anymore. "Your crazy boss is going to torture him. Please, Dad, please!" I can't go on, I'm sobbing so hard.

"Doctor Petrovic is not going to torture any . . . *thing*."

"Get out of my room!"

"You have to trust me, son. This is for the best. Those chemicals you played with are toxic, potentially lethal." He stands. "Needless to say, the cellar is off-limits until all the boxes are removed. I padlocked the grate in case you get any ideas."

As he's closing my bedroom door behind him, I hurl a shoe hard enough to gouge the wood. Beaten, I throw myself facedown, hugging my pillow, and accidentally punch Ella's cap out from underneath.

Nooooooo!

It flies off the bed and skids along the floor until it hits the wall.

I race over and scoop up the cap only to buckle to my knees in despair. Inside, the vial is empty. The stopper got knocked off, spilling out the magic formula. Every last drop of it.

No more green slime.

CHAPTER 34

No slime, no journal.
   No Houdini.

CHAPTER 35

No will to go on.

CHAPTER 36

Crying for hours will only get you a headache.

And I have a bangaroo. It's midafternoon, and I haven't slept since the night before last. I should be happy we're on break, or I'm sure Dad would force me to go to school. I don't even have it in me to see Ella. She came by this morning to go to the skate park, but I told Kyle to get rid of her. She didn't seem to know about Houdini or that the double-crossing Ripper ruined my life. I wonder if she'd give him a pass for that.

A few hours after her, jerk-face himself had the nerve to show up, and if I wasn't paralyzed with grief, I'd have gone down to decimate him. Kyle actually felt sorry for the guy. Said Ripper seemed genuinely remorseful about the whole thing. As if.

I wipe my runny nose and roll over, and when I do, the tape falls out of my pocket. The one from the lab.

05.05.1989 Final Test.

Snatching it off the floor, I bolt downstairs. Dad's at the lab so I burst into his room without knocking. He still has his old camcorder hooked up. I eject *Yosemite Summer '01* and pop in the *Final Test*.

Bracing myself, I hit play. The picture is grainy, lots of dirt on it. Whoever's holding the camera either has shaky hands or thinks he's being artsy. Streetlamps are the main source of light—it's nighttime—but I recognize where they are. Crampus. Crampus in 1989.

Rain hurls down. On the tape, not now. It's the mother of all storms. Lightning shoots across the sky, followed by a drum solo of thunder. The sound is about as good as the picture quality: not very.

Speeding directly toward the camera, a black hearse fishtails on slippery puddles before slamming on the brakes. The car skids to a halt, shockingly close, but the person holding the camera doesn't cower.

Inside the car, Dr. Petrovic wrestles with, then kicks open the sticky door. He's about thirty years younger, if the label on the tape is accurate, but I'd have guessed fifty. The camera operator rushes over to him, holding an umbrella, but the doctor's beige corduroy suit is already soaked through. That's how hard it's raining. His jet-black hair sticks to him like paint. And his pale skin shines with the stormy moisture.

"Ditch the umbrella, Schmelding. You'll need two hands for this."

Schmelding. The Animal Control freak. He releases the umbrella, and a gust of wind takes it away. Lots of jiggling and then the camera tilts 90 degrees. I presume Schmelding attached it to himself like a body cam, but sideways. I tilt my head likewise and continue watching.

Dr. Petrovic opens the back of the hearse, revealing a coffin inside. A fancy one with carvings and gold bars running along both sides. It was probably pretty and shiny at one point but it's dull and dirty with clumps of mud and twigs stuck to it.

Schmelding cracks his knuckles, then presumably his neck as the camera jostles with him. The men each brace a foot on the bumper and pull the coffin out. It lands with a sloshy thud, and the lid pops open. Yep, there's a dead guy in there. The wackadoodle doctor giggles, then jumps on the lid, butt first, closing it with his weight.

The picture abruptly cuts to a grotesque close-up of Schmelding's eyes and nose. He backs up, stepping off a chair, and I see they're in the lab now. The camera is on top of a cabinet—probably the one where I found the tape—giving a wide view of the room.

Dr. Petrovic and his sidekick transfer the corpse from the coffin onto a metal table. The corpse is so fresh, he looks like he's sleeping. Next to that table is another one with a body on it, but this body is alive. It's a woman, strapped down by her wrists, ankles, and forehead. Her eyes dart from side to side as she follows the doctor's every move.

A tray of scalpels, scissors, bone saws, and other gory tools are laid out on a lab cart situated between the corpse and the woman. The leather journal, brand new and smooth with the words *Human Replication and Reanimation* etched on the cover, is next to the tools. Dr. Petrovic opens the book to a page near the end where complex formulas are scribbled on it.

From a small refrigerator, Schmelding retrieves a rack of test tubes. It's amid a collection of petri dishes brimming with disgusting fuzz and several brown-bagged lunches. The rack has six slots, and in each slot is a tube filled with incandescent green slime. The slime that created Houdini.

Without warning, the lunatic doctor starts sawing away on the dead guy's chest, and that's when I start fast-forwarding. Keeping my stomach down while his is coming out is not easy.

Dr. Petrovic guts the corpse, placing each organ in its own glass container filled with slimy, snot-like liquid. He scribbles copious notes throughout the process.

A white streak shoots across the screen, and everything goes dark. Intrigued, I rewind and play at normal speed to see what occurred. It's a bolt of electricity that ping-pongs around the room with a sizzle and buzz. *BOOF.* The lights go out. The woman shrieks. The lab is dimly lit by the flames from a row of Bunsen burners.

Unfazed, the young doctor takes a syringe as large as a turkey baster and fills it with the slime from one of the tubes. Another surge of electricity shoots through the room and zaps the green slime in the syringe. Thunder booms. The gooey substance bubbles. Not only in the syringe, but in the tubes as well, as if all the slime is a single entity. Neither Dr. Petrovic nor Schmelding notice.

Dr. Petrovic positions the giant needle over the woman's frontal lobe, and she screams bloody murder, giving me chills.

Turn it off, turn it off, I beg myself. But I can't. I keep watching.

The lab lights up all of a sudden, startling me enough to jump back, but it's just the overheads; they're back on. The woman stops screaming, and everyone looks over to the door, mood broken. Calm silence.

Standing there, flanked by two security guards, is a young Dean Smith. I recognize the bow tie and bushy eyebrows. He shakes his head, like this is routine.

"How many times, Doctor? How many times must I warn you?"

"You have no vision, Dean Smith," the doctor says. "This is the future."

The dean marches over and unlatches the woman. "Mrs.

Brickelstein, I implore you to stop accepting his invitations. Fool me once . . ."

"Oh, I could never fool you," she says with a cheery smile, missing his point.

The dean sighs. "I'll see you at this year's fundraiser?"

"I'll be there!" Chipper as can be, Mrs. Brickelstein gathers her purse and coat, then waves flirtatiously to Dr. Petrovic. "Till next time."

"No, Mrs. Brickelstein," Dean Smith says.

Dr. Petrovic waves back to her in a "toodles" sort of way.

Fuming, the dean catches his hand to stop him. "First frogs. Then corpses. Then Mrs. Brickelstein. What's next, Doctor? Innocent bystanders? Are students going to start disappearing from campus?"

Hold everything! Did I hear that right? I rewind.

"What's next, Doctor? Innocent bystanders? Are students going to start disappearing from campus?"

I pause the tape, stunned. I can't believe it. Houdini didn't eat all those people. Dr. Petrovic did. Well, he didn't eat them, but he's the attacker. He's the monster!

CHAPTER 37

Ecstatic is an understatement.

The minutes feel like hours, but I stay in Dad's room with the tape cued up. If I've learned anything, it's that I can't trust myself to stay awake no matter how determined I am. And I can't risk missing Dad when he gets home. He works so much, he's hardly ever here.

But after an hour of no Dad, curiosity gets the best of me. I hit play to watch the rest of the tape.

With Mrs. Brickelstein gone, the security guards each grab Dr. Petrovic by an elbow and escort him out as he calls back, "You can't get rid of me this easily, Dean Smith. I have tenure, you know."

Schmelding does an awkward dodgeball shuffle—left, right, left, right—to get around the dean even though the dean's not trying to stop him.

"Get out!" Dean Smith finally shouts, and Schmelding bolts.

A moment later, a burly guy in grass-stained overalls enters and asks what he's supposed to do with all this stuff, and the dean tells him, "Burn it, bury it, do whatever you want. Just get rid of it."

The tape ends. So that's how the stuff got here. A hoarding janitor.

My eyes snap open at the sound of the front door closing.

It's two thirty in the morning. Dad's home.

He checks in on Kyle, who's still up, because I hear muffled conversation. A moment later, he's climbing the next flight of stairs. He'll probably go to check on me now so I hit rewind on the camcorder, then run and open his bedroom door to intercept him.

"Houdini didn't eat anyone," I blurt out as he's approaching the landing.

"Monty. What're you doing in my room?"

"Didn't you hear me? Houdini's innocent. I have proof."

As he enters, Dad's eyes go right to the *Yosemite Summer '01* tape tossed on his bed, and I know that look. Anger. "Did you go through my belongings?"

"Dad, listen to me. I have proof that Houdini didn't eat those people. Dr. Petrovic is the one who attacked them."

I'm hyped up, ready to defend my point, but Dad's expression flips from heated to sorrowful in a blink—throwing me off my game—and he takes my hands compassionately. "Oh, Monty . . ."

"Stop it." I pull my hands away. "Why do you do that?"

"Do what? Care about you?"

"Treat me like I'm delusional. You did that when I told you about Houdini, and he was real. And you're doing it again."

"You're emotional. I understand. You miss him. But do you

hear yourself? You're accusing a renowned, award-winning scientist of killing his own students."

A terrible grinding noise shocks my ears, and I swing my eyes over to the camcorder, remembering I left it on rewind. "No. No, no, no." My proof.

Dad rushes to the camcorder, snatching it up before I can move. "I'm going to be very upset if you destroyed one of my tapes, Montague. They're irreplaceable. I can't get those back." He sounds like he's going to cry, until he sees the label. "Final test? What is this?"

He hits eject to pop out the tape, but it's caught on something, and he unspools the entire thing as he removes it from the camcorder. I fall to my knees, screaming in torment. Inside my head. In real life, I stand immobilized by despair.

"This is why you don't use other people's things without asking," he says, holding up the tangled mess. Completely unaware of my despondency. "I would've told you the rewind doesn't work properly. You have to manually stop it."

Nothing left to say, I turn to leave, hopeless.

"Hold on a second, young man. What is this? Where'd you get it?"

"I found it in the lab. It's of Dr. Petrovic experimenting on a corpse and a Mrs. Brickelstein, but Dean Smith shut him down because he was concerned it would lead to experimenting on students. No, he didn't admit to chopping up students," I answer before Dad can ask. "And no, I can't say for sure he stole the dead guy without permission, and yes, Mrs. Brickelstein seemed perfectly happy to be there."

I about-face and leave, going straight to my room like a zombie, alive but dead.

CHAPTER 38

It's 7 a.m.

With Dad in the shower and Kyle still in bed, I'm out the door before either has a chance to discover I'm gone. Poor Watson didn't understand why he wasn't coming with me, but some things are too hard to explain to a dog.

I skate faster than the morning traffic, reaching the university in a record-breaking three minutes. I ditch my board by the administration building, hiding it in a bush, and stroll as if I'm not in a panic trying to save my best friend's life. The security guard lets me into the building, no questions asked. It helps that I'm carrying what looks like my science fair project but in reality is a piece of plywood with random wires and dead batteries glued to it.

The project hits the trash once I reach the basement, and I sprint toward Dr. Petrovic's torture chamber. The halls are quiet. Spring Break. I peek through the window on the door to see what I'm dealing with. Schmelding's near the door, his back to me, and he's blocking most of my view of the lab. His Taser is holstered on his tool belt, and his hand rests on it, at the ready. That worries me for Houdini, so I open the door to throw myself on the grenade.

"Hi," I say.

Schmelding jumps, squeezing the Taser unintentionally, but only zapping the floor. Dr. Petrovic, scalpel in hand, spins away from whatever he was doing, toward me, and I see Houdini for the first time since his capture. He's skinny. Losing so much hair. His big brown eyes droop with sadness, and I can't tell if he even knows who I am.

There's a cage in the corner, but he's not in it. Clearly, he's too weak to move, let alone fight for his freedom. He's in what looks like a scarier version of a dentist chair equipped with arm and leg restraints, but they're not being used. A rubber cap with cables coming out of it is also attached to the chair and not in use. What is being utilized is a magnifying glass positioned over Houdini's forearm to amplify various marks on him from being stabbed. Sliced. Scraped.

Rage hits me like an earthquake, my whole body tremoring, but I have to be smart.

"Montague," Dr. Petrovic says with a welcoming smile. He's lost another tooth. "The young man I was hoping to see. Come, come. Don't dillydally."

I make my way over, and Schmelding is on me like sweat, only smellier. Surprisingly, Dr. Petrovic lets me take Houdini's hand.

"It's me, Houdini. I'm here." I hug him.

Houdini blinks, understanding me, but it's so labored. Even blinking is too difficult for him.

"As you can see, Montague, our little experiment is not faring well."

"He's not an experiment. He's my friend."

"Semantics, dear boy," the doctor says. "Either way, he

won't last. Not without your cooperation. You see, his genetic makeup consists of a component I cannot identify. Of course, I calculated your DNA into the equation." He plucks a hair from my head.

"Stop doing that."

"For safekeeping," he says. "But there's something else, a foreign substance that infiltrated the original serum over these past thirty years. If you care at all about him, you'll return my serum."

"Well, if you care about not going to jail, you'll let him go right now."

"Jail?" The doctor laughs, and his lackey echoes him.

"I found your tape," I say in a deadly serious tone. "I know what you did all those years ago. In nineteen eighty-nine. Stealing dead bodies, cutting them open. And now, attacking students. I have proof. And if you don't let Houdini go, I'll give it to the cops. I swear I will."

The doctor yanks me toward him. To stab my brain with his scalpel, I'm sure. He gets in two kisses on my cheeks before I squirm out of his grasp, leaving his third kiss in the air.

What? Ugh. Gross. I can't wipe my face fast enough.

"I've been searching for that tape for decades, Montague." He turns to Schmelding, clapping ecstatically. "The elements are coming together, Schmelding. The serum, the journal, the final test recording."

With them celebrating, I squeeze Houdini's hand to signal him as I whisper, "Run."

Dr. Petrovic is a lightning rod of speed and latches onto Houdini's other arm. "Tut-tut," he warns.

"Let go!"

The madman does the exact opposite, and pulls Houdini away from me, stretching him across the room.

"No, please." Anguished, I don't know what to do, but I can't hurt my friend like this. I release my hold, and Houdini rebounds into Dr. Petrovic, knocking him off balance. Schmelding runs to catch the doctor before he topples, and I scramble for Houdini, but I'm grabbed from behind and held back.

"Monty," Dad shouts in my ear. He's got me pinned like a straightjacket.

"Put me down!" I writhe and kick, struggling to free myself.

"Calm down and I will."

I stop fighting, and he releases me to the floor but keeps a hold of my wrist.

"How can you torture Houdini like this? How can you be so cruel?"

"We're merely collecting skin cells, Monty, nothing more. It doesn't hurt. Please try to understand that we need to identify his genetic makeup in order to help him get better."

"You're the reason he's sick. Don't you see? If you'd let him come home, he'd be fine."

"It doesn't work that way."

"Please, Dad."

"Monty, stop. This isn't a child's game. This creature is suffering—"

"Because of you!"

"Stop it!" Dad yells with clenched fists. "We're doing everything we can. You're just going to have to trust me on that."

"No!" I pull free and race toward Houdini, but Dad hoists me up before I get there, and carries me away.

Crying, I reach for Houdini, and he reaches for me too but is too weak to do anything else. A tear rolls down his face and a tuft of fur floats off his shoulder, and that's the last I see of him as Dad hauls me out of the lab. My head drops in despair as everything inside me dies.

CHAPTER 39

His betrayal leaves me numb.

All my fighting, all my crying and screaming, all my pleading from the bottom of my heart means nothing to Dad. I can't even muster anger anymore.

"How could you do this to me?" I say quietly. "I hate you."

Dad lets go. Guess I said the magic words. He looks shocked, but I don't care. I meant it. I hate him. I walk away and don't look back.

I'm tortured by the thought of Houdini being trapped, experimented on, heartbroken. Wondering how I could let them do this to him. How I could not protect him. The weight of my sorrow exhausts me, and I stumble into one of the labs, falling against the wall, and slide to the floor.

As I stare off absently, I come to realize my gaze is on the refrigerator that Ashanta had an affinity for. There's a window on the door, and though I can barely move, I drag myself over and peer in. I gasp, shocked back to life. Looking me in the face is another face. A human face. A man, to be precise; all of him, not just his head. A real-life cryogenically frozen specimen waiting to come back. It's official. Everything that goes on in this building is horrible.

I break into a run and don't stop until I make it all the way home, up the stairs, and safely into my bedroom. Watson's glad to see me, and I throw my arms around him, welcoming the comfort. Next thing I know, the morning sun burns my eyes like a ray gun.

I reek worse than Houdini ever did.

My clothes are three days old, and I haven't showered or brushed my teeth in at least that long. But I don't care. The few hours' sleep is like a rebirth of energy and optimism. I bolt out of my room and down the stairs, knocking Kyle out of my way in the foyer as I beeline for the door. My plan is simple: ambush Schmelding when he goes to the bathroom, steal his Taser, and break Houdini out. Zap anyone who gets in my way, Dad included.

Kyle grabs my arm, sending my feet in the air as he yanks me back. I'd fall on my butt, but he's got a tight grip, keeping me from wiping out entirely.

"Let go," I demand.

"Make me."

"Real mature."

"I know I am, but what are you?"

"Kyle!"

"Monty!"

"Stop it. I'm not in the mood."

"Shocker," Kyle says. He's still got the kung-fu grip on my arm. "Dad wants me to keep an eye on you. As in, don't let you out of my sight."

"What for?"

"You tell me, butt-wipe."

As if. Knowing Kyle, he'll side with Dad. I try a different tactic. "You gonna hold my arm all day or what?" He lets go. "Thank you."

I take a step toward the living room, then spin and make a break for it. He yanks me back by my shirt this time.

"Hey!"

"You can't outrun me and you can't outsmart me, so you might as well tell me what you did that has Dad all peeved now."

"I'm trying to save my friend, okay? He needs me. He's sick. And Dad and those crazy scientists are doing all sorts of cruel experiments on him because they don't care about him. They're heartless monsters."

"I'm sure Dad isn't doing anything that'll hurt your freak of nature."

"You didn't see him, Kyle. Houdini was scared. His fur was falling off. His eyes looked so sad." Emotion cuts off my vocal cords, taking my voice.

Kyle puts a comforting hand on my shoulder. "Dad's not a monster, Monty. You know that. Whatever he's doing, he's doing it for Houdini. You have to trust him."

I pull away. "Forget it. I don't know why I thought I could count on you. You never take my side."

I march upstairs. On my own, like always.

CHAPTER 40

It's padlocked, all right.

Not that I expected Dad to bluff about locking the grate to the cellar. But I have bolt cutters. Clearly, he forgot I lost the key to my bike's U-lock last year and we had to cut it free. A dim light is on down there, probably the bulb over the lab area, but my heart aches for it to be Houdini. Escaped and waiting for me.

I snip the shank and release the lock from the grate, letting the metal ladder unfold. Grabbing the outside bars, I slide all the way down into the cellar.

"Houdini?" I call in a whisper. Even though I knew he wouldn't really be here, I'm still crushed he doesn't appear.

The lab has been boxed up. All the equipment and potions are sealed away in the crates, I assume. Not a petri dish in sight. The metal tables are wiped clean, almost sparkling.

I climb over the crates and access the steps going up to the doors that lead to the outside. The gap is big enough to fit my bolt cutters through, and I clip the chains on the exterior handles. I'm free.

To cover my tracks, I close the doors and wrap the chains around the handle, hiding the broken link. Military-style, I crawl through the backyard and escape through a hole in the fence.

Once out, I sprint toward the university, and get ambushed by Ripper. Not physically, but he emerges from behind a tree, blocking my path.

I'm livid, but don't have time to deal with him now. "Get out of my way."

"Dude, let me explain."

"Explain? Explain how you set me up? Used me? Put my friend's life at risk?"

"I swear, my grandpa promised he wouldn't hurt him."

I shove him. "Well, I guess you're both liars then!"

He doesn't come at me. Instead, he looks remorseful. "What was I supposed to do, Monty? He said nobody would have to die anymore, that my parents would still be alive if the school didn't take away all his stuff. Houdini was proof his research was a success and should continue."

I refuse to give that two-faced weasel any benefit of the doubt. "If you don't get out of my way right now, I'll smash your face in."

"Where you going? Let me help."

That's it! I haul back and swing with all my might, aiming to break that perfect nose again. Ripper catches my fist, inches from his face, and holds me at bay. I kick him in the shin—it's all I have in my arsenal—and he releases my fist with a pained grunt.

"C'mon, Monty."

"Get out of my face! Don't you get it? I'll never forgive you for what you did."

Ripper finally steps aside to let me pass. "I'm really sorry," he says. "Honest. I didn't mean for this to happen."

I take off again toward the university.

No one thought to tell the guard to ban me, so I walk in with a smile and a wave.

It's the hardest thing I've had to do in a long time, fake a smile when I'm dying inside. I take the stairs to the basement and go directly to the men's room closest to Dr. Petrovic's lab. After two hours of camping out in a stall with my feet on the toilet bowl, Dad enters and goes to the urinal. He doesn't pee, though. Not that I'm peeking through the gap in the door—I don't want to send him vibes to look over—but I can see his feet, motionless, yet no unzipping. No stream.

Is he crying?

He is.

Automatically, my stomach sinks and my eyes prickle with tears. I have that feeling I had when I first heard him cry for Mom. Whatever it is, I know it's bad because Dad is an expert at seeing the bright side to everything. Mom's cancer was the one thing that beat him, but that was years ago and he bounced back. Well, the way someone bounces back after the person they love dies.

My wrath dissipates like pollen on a windy day, and all I can think is that he needs me.

As I'm about to reveal myself, Schmelding barrels in, farting loudly. "This might get messy," he tells Dad and takes the stall next to me.

"It's all yours." Dad leaves.

Schmelding's pants drop around his ankles, and my eyes go right to the Taser on his utility belt. Still perched on the toilet seat, leg bouncing with nerves, I wait for him to get started so he'll be in the utmost awkward situation when I make my move. After several prolonged grunts, the floodgates open and he stinks up the joint. I jump from the toilet and reach under the stall before I chicken out. He grabs my wrist and I scream involuntarily, but I've got a good grip on the Taser and I'm able to yank myself free, Taser in hand. I bolt for the exit.

Schmelding bangs into the stall door as he fumbles to make himself decent enough to give chase, but I'm halfway down the corridor before he makes it out of the bathroom.

Panting, I tear into the lab, holding the Taser like a movie villain. "Nobody move," I say.

Dr. Petrovic looks up from whatever it is he's doing to an organ, Ashanta looks up from her computer, and Dad looks up from inside the cage where he's giving Houdini a sponge bath. The cage has been transformed into a cozy-looking bedroom, but it's still a cage. Houdini smiles and my heart melts.

"He's coming with me," I say.

Schmelding races in, skidding to a halt as I swing my aim at him. "Stay back."

"Take care of this, Robbie, Bobbie, Boo," Dr. Petrovic says, returning his attention to the organ.

Dad cradles Houdini's cheek affectionately, whispering to him. I don't hear what he says, but Houdini sighs warmly in response.

"Monty." Dad leaves the cage, approaching me, but I hold my aim. He softens. "Son."

Adrenaline courses through every vein, and my arms shake. I can practically touch him with the Taser. His eyes are red, I think from crying. He looks as sad as Houdini. "Give me the Taser, Monty." Truthfully, he could take it from me at this point, but he doesn't. "I know it's hard losing someone you love—"

"Stop."

"Monty . . ."

"No! He's not dying. I won't let him."

"Monty . . ." Even Dad can't steady his trembling lips. "Some things are out of our control, but Houdini's best chances are here with us. Please believe me, no one wants him to die. *I* don't want him to die. We're working day and night to recreate the serum. And we're close, very close. But he needs us to help him."

Doesn't anyone understand? "He'd be fine if you just let him come home."

"You know that's not true." He's referring to Mom, when she came home. "Love is wonderful, Monty, but it doesn't cure everything."

My soul crumbles to pieces. I drop my arms, letting the Taser swing by my side. Schmelding snatches it from me, but Dad pulls me in for a hug. "I'm sorry, son. Truly."

CHAPTER 41

The vending machines hum.

The overhead fluorescent bulbs hum. My brain hums. My world is white noise. Dad's talking. Ashanta's by his side, supporting him. Or me. I'm not sure who. The cafeteria is empty except for us. A package of Hostess Sno Balls, the pink ones, is on the table before me, along with a hot chocolate.

My ears pop and I hear words. "Great strides . . . replicating formula . . . close . . ." But I don't care that Dad's talking, I don't care what he's saying. I have to know.

"Are you trying to bring Mom back?"

He stops in his tracks. Stunned. "What?"

"Are you trying to bring Mom back from the dead? Because that's the only reason I can think that would make sense for you being so awful, for torturing Houdini by keeping him from me. For using him as a way to get people to give you money to keep doing these unspeakable things. That you think all these experiments will somehow bring Mom back."

"Monty . . ."

"Is that why you're doing this?"

"No."

I turn to Ashanta. "It's why you're doing it, isn't it?"

Dad's thrown by my accusation, I can tell. He's about to come to her defense, but she beats him to it.

"Yes," she says. "Yes."

The room falls silent. Dad didn't know. "I don't understand," he says.

"Jeff," she tells him. "It's been almost eight months. We knew it was coming, much like you did. Nothing we did helped, so we contacted Doctor Petrovic. We were desperate. Jeff agreed to donate his body to this research, and I started working with Dr. Petrovic. Jeff's cryogenically preserved, and this formula is his best hope. If we can replicate his own healthy tissue, we can bring him back."

"So you kill one life to save another," I say. "What gives you the right to decide that one life is more important than another?"

"That's never been our intention, Monty," Ashanta says. "Our research focused solely on donors, not live specimens, for the very purpose of saving lives. But Houdini is a phenomenon. We can't simply disregard him. It would be negligent. I know it's hard to understand, but sometimes we have to make difficult decisions for the greater good."

"I understand perfectly. Your definition of *good* is a lot different than mine." I leave the Sno Balls and hot chocolate on the table and exit.

CHAPTER 42

My heart is a brick.

Once they reveal Houdini at the fundraiser tomorrow, if he lives that long, he'll be gone from my life forever. Even in the best-case scenario—if they replicate the formula and heal him—the university will never give him back to me, not once people know about him. He'll be just another science experiment for them to parade around for their own greed. Locked up in a cage for the rest of his life. How can I be the only one who cares about him?

Usually when the world beats me down, Watson cheers me up, but not even he can lift my spirits. He had big shoes to fill after Mom died, and he never complained about it. If I ever needed to talk, he was there. If I needed a hug, he was happy to oblige. Mom probably knew she was dying when she brought him home for me. She was smart like that. She'd never separate me and Houdini. She understood love, real love.

And magic.

The thought makes me smile. I roll to my side and look at her picture on the floor next to my bed. Whenever we had a problem, we pulled out our top hats and props, and by the time we were done, our problems disappeared. Like magic.

Sure, it was an illusion, but isn't that what magic is, anyway? Illusion.

I bolt upright. Great Kalamazoo! That's it!

My brain fires in all directions, a traffic jam of thoughts. I grab a pencil and pad and spend two hours mapping out the campus from memory, estimating how long it'll take to get from points A to B to C to Freedom with all the necessary components. Next, I write a list of equipment so I won't forget anything when nerves take over (more than they are now). Plan in place, I get to the meat of it. Making rabbits disappear.

Orville stares up at me, nose twitching.

My face is pressed into the metal bars on the top of his cage. Dried saliva crusts my chin. I must've fallen asleep. It's still dark outside, which means I didn't waste the entire night dozing. Light-headed from exhaustion, I push myself upright, trying to remember where I left off. On the bed, Watson spoons Snowball, but Smore is nowhere.

Smore!

I remember now. I made him disappear. For real. In a million years, I couldn't reproduce that trick if I tried, nor would I want to. The idea is to create an illusion. You don't actually make them disappear.

A knock on the door startles me into a scream, and Dad enters, like that's an invitation.

"Monty?" He relaxes when he sees I'm fine, but now I'm tense because he's got Smore.

"What're you doing with Smore? You gonna experiment on him too?"

"He was on the porch. You shouldn't leave him outside alone."

I take Smore and put him in the cage with Orville.

"Why are you still up?" Dad says. "It's midnight."

"Can you leave, please?"

"In a second. I want to talk to you about Houdini."

I fight the instant burn of tears forming as my insides suffocate me in distress. He's gotten weaker. Or worse.

"We think we've replicated the original serum from Doctor Petrovic's journal," Dad says, lifting my spirits. "But bear in mind the formula that created Houdini might, in itself, be temporary. Or Houdini might have a short life span. Or maybe an illness that can't be cured."

"He isn't sick, he's sad. It's possible to die of a broken heart, you know?"

"If that were true, Monty, I'd have died."

"No. Because you had us, and we had you. That's why we were okay. Houdini has no one. He doesn't understand why you're doing this to him. You'd lose your will to live too if you were locked up and poked and prodded. Just bring him home."

"He needs the serum."

"He needs *me!*" *I need him.*

"If I thought bringing him home would work, I'd do it in a second. But life is more complicated than love and magic tricks."

"How would you know? You never tried either."

"Monty . . ." Dad says consolingly. "I'm sorry I couldn't save Mom."

"And I'm sorry it wasn't you instead of her."

"Me too," he says, dropping his head. "Me too." He leaves.

CHAPTER 43

I put on my cape.

Kyle's at Diego's house, and Dad's on his way to the fundraiser. I have my backpack of tricks, my skateboard, and my stomach full of butterflies. Like a cat burglar, I wear all black and sneak into the darkness of night. A shopping bag on the porch trips me, but I manage to stumble over it without falling. My heart races at what might be inside. Houdini's ear or finger or eye as a warning to return the original slime (that I no longer have!).

I peek into the bag. It's the skirt. Kyle's. On top is a piece of paper with an *XO* on it. I shove it closer to the door, telling myself to stick to PG movies from now on. Before I make it past our property, Zippy and Elmo casually step out from behind a huge oak tree.

"If it ain't our trusted lookout," Zippy says.

My butterflies turn to lead. "My dad's right inside, guys."

Zippy pins me to the oak, his forearm pressed against my throat. "Really? Who was the Poindexter just left in a tux?"

"I'm sorry, okay? I didn't see the cops. It's not like I do this for a living."

"Wrong answer," Elmo says.

"Everyone makes mistakes," Ripper says, startling us as he ollies out of the shadows.

Zippy mock shudders. "Ooh. There's two of them."

"Better count again, brah." It's Thrash this time. He and that other guy whose name I really need to learn skate over.

Elmo smirks. "Four."

"And a half," Zippy adds with a laugh when Ella joins them. Unintimidated, he turns his attention back to me. "Payback's a bitch, kid."

"Who're you calling 'kid'?" That's Kyle now, approaching from across the street. Diego's with him.

"This ain't your business, man," Elmo says, puffing his chest.

"This is more than my business. Man. This is my brother." Kyle physically removes Zippy's arm from my neck, freeing me. It helps that he's bigger than Zippy. "You mess with him, you mess with me."

Zippy tries to stare him down, but Kyle doesn't flinch. Zippy breaks. "Pshh." He nods to Elmo, and they saunter off, acting like they're not scared.

When they disappear around the corner, I spin to Kyle and the others. "What? So now I'm supposed to thank everyone?"

"Take it easy," Kyle says.

"No! This doesn't make up for all the times you were mean to me. And you," I say, pointing to Ripper, "nothing will make up for what you did. You're a backstabbing, two-faced, lying bully who made my life miserable. Now get out of my way, all of you. I have a real friend who needs me."

"Monty," Ella says, tempering my fury with her voice. "We

are your friends. Let us help. You can't bust Houdini out by yourself."

I glare at Ripper. Who else did he blab to?

"Everyone's gonna know about Houdini after tonight," he says. "There's no point in keeping it a secret anymore. What we need to do now is band together for him, so put aside your stupid pride. You can hate me later."

I'm torn between wrath and a flicker of hope.

"Plus," Ella adds, "it's gonna be really awkward to see you in Spanish Club if you don't let us help."

Kyle puts an arm around me. "What do you say, butt-wipe?"

They're right. I need them. "Let's go ruin a party."

CHAPTER 44

Tuxedos and gowns.

This gala's a big deal. The campus is teeming with snooty-looking grown-ups mingling with one another, taking their time to file into the Communications building. I don't see anyone I know—except Mrs. Brickelstein, but she doesn't know me—so we could conceivably stroll into the Science building without suspicion and get this thing in motion. But tonight's too important to take any chances. We stay back.

Communications is the next building over from the Science building. Sometimes you're lucky that way. I laid out my plan to the others earlier, and none of them expressed confidence in it, but it's the best one I got, and now that we're seven strong— me, Kyle, Diego, Ripper, Thrash, Ella, and Chen (that's the other guy's name)—I'm downright giddy about it. Not just because Ella's part of the seven. But it helps.

According to Dad's calendar, the fundraiser was set to start at 7:00 p.m., and it's already 7:45. Guess adults don't have to play by the same rules as us. Show up five minutes late to class, and it's detention for you.

"Did you really get accepted to another school?" I whisper to Kyle.

He shrugs like it's no big deal. "Just some rinky-dink outfit in Cambridge."

"Yale?"

"Harvard, you dope."

Same thing. "Why didn't you tell me?"

"So you could hold it against me that I like being around my kid brother?"

Darn. Serious lump in my throat. "Your skirt's back, by the way."

"Cool." After a moment, he says, "Is it weird?"

I shrug. "You're asking the guy who wears a cape."

He nods, amused.

Ripper brings us back to our plan. "Looks like everyone's gone in."

No gowns or tuxedos in sight. I want to vomit. What was I thinking? This is the stupidest idea on the planet. I can't do this.

"You got this," Kyle says.

I nod—at least I think I do; I'm numb with nerves—and we split up as planned. Kyle and Diego head to the Communications building. Ripper, Thrash, Ella, and Chen come with me to the Science building. I look over my shoulder at Kyle, and he's looking back at me. With a smile, he gives me a thumbs-up, and my butterflies scatter. I can do this.

The fluorescent lights crackle.

With the gala in full swing, the Science building is abandoned. Not even the security guard is here. Luckily, Ripper has keys, because all I had to get in was a story about my Dad needing his cryogen specimen ASAP for the presentation.

Ella is stationed on the first floor, half inside the stairwell, half outside, so she can keep an eye on the entrance to the building as well as the elevators midway down the main corridor. Chen is the lookout at the bottom of the stairs, half in, half out, so he can communicate with both Ella and us. Us being Ripper, Thrash, and me.

Smoke wafts out from under the doors of several labs in the basement, presumably from ongoing experiments. I head for the gold: Mr. Popsicle.

Ripper stretches his neck to look in the window on the freezer door. "Is he dead?"

"Technically," I say.

"Let me see." Thrash pushes Ripper aside. "Whoa."

"This is exactly why we have to get Houdini away from your lunatic grandfather," I say to Ripper, adding, "No offense."

He shrugs like it doesn't bother him. "Will he defrost when we unplug him?"

"Doubt it. It takes overnight to thaw a turkey, and he's gotta be ten times that size."

"Way to ruin turkey, brah," Thrash says.

I unlock the wheels, and we roll the freezer into the corridor. Chen darts into the stairwell for his signal from Ella and returns with a thumbs-up. We steer the freezer to the elevator down the corridor. I push the button incessantly until Ripper grabs my hand to stop me.

"Dude" is all he says.

He's right; I need to calm down. But you'd think this building has fifty stories for as long as it's taking. Too much time is dangerous, and now I'm positive someone else is here. Someone on the third floor—probably that Schmelding freak—

and that's why the elevator is taking so long. It had to go up before coming down and—*DING!*

My heart jumps.

The doors open.

Empty.

The three of us push the freezer in, and as I'm about to press the button to the first floor, the elevator drops. We scream, but the safety catches immediately, cutting us off.

Ripper laughs. "Relax. How far down can it go anyway? We're already in the basement."

The elevator doors start to close, and Thrash juts his arm out, stopping them. "Yeah, but do you want to be trapped in an elevator with a dead guy?"

"Take the stairs," I say. "Meet us up there."

After a beat, Thrash retreats his arm, letting the doors close with him still inside. All for one and one for all. I press the button to the first floor, and the elevator grinds its way up. Slowly. Very slowly. None of us speaks for fear our voices might tip the scales and send us plummeting.

The doors open to Ella and Chen, both looking relieved. "Dang," she says. "I've never heard an elevator work so hard."

"Yeah, duh, so get out of the way," Thrash says.

Amused, they scatter, giving us room to roll the freezer out. The car bounces up from its own relief once the weight is gone, and Ella and Chen vie to get a peek of Mr. Popsicle.

"He looks strange," Chen says. "Is he supposed to be puke yellow?"

Now we all squeeze in to get a look. He is sallower than I remember. And that protrusion on his left cheek, was that always there? As we're staring at him, his eyes pop wide open.

"Agh!" is the general consensus as we stumble back. Recovering quickly, I rush to get another look, dreading that I might've brought Mr. Popsicle back to life-ish.

His eyes are closed. "Probably a reflex," I tell everyone. "Happens all the time when you die. Your body twitches and stuff."

"And farts too, I heard," says Chen.

"Ew." Ella punches him in the shoulder. "You just cut one."

Chen laughs. "Not me. It was the dead guy."

"Knock it off," Ripper says, obviously sensing my nerves. "This is serious."

Everyone hushes and nods, looking solemn. The halls are completely quiet.

Chen farts again, piercing the silence with a sharp squeaky trill.

This time we all giggle.

Then burst into uncontrollable laughter, like it was the funniest thing in the world. That's what happens when you're under extreme pressure. The silliest thing can pop the cork.

Feeling a little more at ease, we continue our operation, rolling the freezer out the rear of the building, where there are no stairs to contend with, and over to the rear of the Communications building, where Kyle has left the door ajar for us.

CHAPTER 45

Dean Smith is at the podium stage left.

Guests are drinking, laughing, anticipating. There must be thirty huge round tables with at least ten place settings at each one. All occupied. Crystal, china, crisp white linens. The kind of thing you see at weddings or in the movies. On a school day, this would be the studio where journalist majors do fake broadcasts, but tonight, it's dressed for money.

Center stage is a freestanding curtain about ten feet tall and wide, and I know Houdini's back there. I'm desperate to see him, to tell him I'm here, but there's no time. I stay hidden in the shadows, backstage. Sweat soaks my neck and armpits.

Dad sits beside Ashanta at the table nearest the steps leading up to the podium. Dr. Petrovic hovers between their table and the one next to them, madder than usual as he smiles, nods, and measures the size of guests' heads with his fingers. Not subtle at all.

"Welcome, esteemed guests," Dean Smith begins. "You've all been invited here this evening to witness a very special discovery by Clear Rock University's respected team of scientists."

Liar! Liar, liar, liar!

"The research has taken decades of hard work and dedication, but tonight, you will see it was well worth the effort. Allow me to introduce the team. Doctor Robert Hyde."

Dad stands to acknowledge the applause, and I hate him more now than ever.

"Doctor Ashanta Richards-Mitchell." She also stands, smiling to the room.

"And of course, the irrefutable, Doctor Petr Petrovic."

Applause, applause, applause.

Dr. Petrovic addresses the crowd. "You have all been very patient. Therefore, I will only say that what you are about to behold . . ." His gaze settles on the gleaming head of a bald man, and he's mesmerized.

"Doctor?" Dad says, and the dazed doc snaps to.

"Manners, Robbie, Bobbie, Boo." Dr. Petrovic addresses the room again. "As I was saying, what you are about to behold is a scientific achievement that will change life as we know it." He swoops his arm toward the stage. "Behold my creation!"

The curtain drops, and a collective gasp fills the room.

Houdini, my sweet friend, is slumped in a cage, for show; he's obviously too weak to be any kind of threat. Nearly hairless, his ribs stick out prominently. His big brown eyes sag sorrowfully. He tries to smile for the guests, and they recoil in fear and revulsion, some shrieking. I want to cry and yell at them at the same time for their reaction, but instead, I jet out of the shadows with a performer's smile on my face.

It's showtime!

CHAPTER 46

Houdini brightens, and my world is right again.

I lean in, whispering, "I meant it when I said you could count on me."

"Montague Hyde. What are you doing?"

Oh, that's right. Dad's here. And glaring at me. Next to him, Ashanta looks perplexed, and Dr. Petrovic looks fascinated in the wonky eye and horrified in the other.

"Magic tricks, for starters."

I whip out my wand and turn it into a bouquet of flowers, then hand it to the woman closest to me. The audience seems confused but intrigued and no longer appalled. A few of them clap. My first applause. Houdini joins in, bolstering my resolve.

"Nothing up my sleeve . . ." I say, proving it.

The audience watches, rapt. Dad fumes, lips pursed, but he's not one to make a scene. From my sleeve, I pull and pull and pull and pull until—ta-da!—I've got one giant scarf. Actually, it's the string of scarves Houdini pulled from his sleeve when he did the trick, but I sewed them into one big square. The audience applauds. Except Dad, who chews on his nail and bounces his leg.

I slide my eyes over to Ripper, Ella, Thrash, and Chen, who are backstage with Mr. Popsicle. How I thought I could do this on my own is a testament to the delusions of heartbreak. I'm lucky to have a group of friends on board.

I throw the massive scarf over Houdini's cage, covering it entirely. "Abracadabra, Kalamazoo," I recite as I circle the cage, waving my hand dramatically. "Roses are red, and your faces are too."

I yank away the scarf, and Houdini is gone.

I did it! Well, we did it.

Murmurs circulate the room. Dad jumps to his feet. "That's enough, Monty. Bring him back."

As if obliging, I throw the scarf over the cage. "Abracadabra, Kalamazoo."

I wait a beat, because the lights are supposed to go out, but they don't. My smile hardens. Everyone stares at me, anticipating the reveal.

Stalling, I dramatically circle the cage as though it's part of the act, emoting, "Abracadabra. Kalamazoo."

Backstage, hidden from the guests, Kyle waves his arms frantically at Diego, who's in the lighting booth.

"I SAID—"

The lights go out. Pitch black. Shrieks and cries circulate. Shuffling and scuffling onstage and off.

"Montague," Dad yells from the darkness.

There's a fleshy collision and more scrambling—unexpected—but I continue as if everything is going according to plan.

"Hold on to your bladders, ladies and gents," I call out amid the chaos. "One great scientific creation deserves another. Abracadabra, Kalam—"

The lights go on.

Darn it, Diego. He was supposed to count to ten after I finished my recitation, giving me time to flee the building. At least I cleared the stage before his goof, and I duck in the shadows.

Pulse racing, I remove my cape and check the lining. Furry-ish. Fleshy. Houdini! I wasn't sure he'd have the strength to "disappear" into my cape after everything he's been through. He stares at me with the happiest eyes—*doink, doink*—and I want to hug him, but there's no time. We have to get out of here, and it's going to be a lot harder with the lights on.

I put my finger to my lips and motion to our exit route. Houdini nods, understanding, then flings himself into my arms anyway. Heart-warmed, I return the hug.

"Okay, let's go," I whisper.

An outburst of terrified shrieks stops me, and I look back. Dad's onstage, having removed the scarf, and is doubled over in disbelief.

Mr. Popsicle is in the cage instead of Houdini. That was the trick—a simple distraction to give me a head start. But he's not frozen anymore. He's a hideous mutation. Veins pulsate out of his yellow skin, and he froths at the mouth.

Ashanta faints. I feel nauseous. I didn't mean to wake the dead. Honest.

Mr. Popsicle kicks the door off the cage and pounces like a panther, charging the crowd. Panic. Mass evacuation. Trampling. Screaming. Fleeing for their lives. Dr. Petrovic snaps his fingers and Schmelding appears by his side, loading a dart gun.

This wasn't how it was supposed to go down, but I can't stop now. I split!

CHAPTER 47

Lightning rips open the black sky.

The roll of thunder drowns out the mayhem I left behind. Rain splatters off my wheels as I skate like a maniac with the frail Houdini on my back. Several blocks ahead of us, Ripper, Ella, Thrash, and Chen disperse, going to their respective homes. Before we put the plan in motion, I made them promise they'd leave as soon as Houdini was out of his prison. I couldn't live with myself if they got in trouble for helping me.

Kyle and Diego were supposed to take off right after the lights came back up, but I was too overwhelmed by the chaos to check if Kyle was still backstage. Hopefully not. Dad was angrier than the Hulk. But he'll calm down once he realizes Houdini just needs to be with me (and out of that cage) to get healthy again.

In preparation, I hid a duffel bag with three days' worth of food, some blankets, and a gallon of water in the bushes by the skate park. Not that I'm planning on staying there—it's too close to the university—but it was the most convenient place to store supplies.

When I arrive at the stash, I unwrap Houdini's arms from around my neck, and he flops to the ground.

"Houdini?"

He lies there, still as can be.

I gently shake him. "Houdini?"

He doesn't stir.

No, no, no. I shake harder. "Please, Houdini, please wake up."

Nothing.

"Houdini! Please! Wake up!" I shake him frantically, but he's a lifeless mound. My chest constricts with pain. What happened? I freed him. He's with me. He should be fine. *Someone help me.*

A bolt of lightning sails across the sky like a shooting star and strikes an antenna on the roof of the Communications building, showering sparks down on the Science building.

Soaked through to my guts, shivering from failure, I stare at the building, ominous in the torrential rain, and realize I was wrong. Love isn't the answer. Houdini needs the serum.

CHAPTER 48

The elevator doors open with a hiss.

The familiar crackle of fluorescent tubes comforts me for some reason. With Houdini draped around my neck like a scarf, I skate toward the lab where Mr. Popsicle resided. What I really need is in Dr. Petrovic's lab, but I can't bring Houdini there. I need to keep him hidden from that mad scientist.

A metal table shoved in the corner of Mr. Popsicle's lab appears big enough to accommodate Houdini's size. It's on the same wall as the door, so if anyone peers in the window on the door, they won't be able to see him.

Laying him on the table, I realize how cold his body is, but he's not shivering. He's not moving at all, except for the shallowest of breaths. Time is of the essence, but I need to hug him once more.

"I'm so sorry, Houdini. If I knew you needed their serum, I wouldn't have broken you out. I'll find some. Just hang on, okay? For me."

Loath to leave his side, I don't look back as I head for the door for fear of changing my mind. The hallways are quiet. I run all the way to Dr. Petrovic's lab in the next corridor and peek in to make sure no one's there. All clear. I enter.

The cage they kept Houdini in is still here. They used a different one for their fundraiser. The floor inside the cage is covered in his hair. All sorts of tubes and IVs are outside the bars, and I think of all the times poor Houdini was hooked up to various things, not understanding why. The sourness in my stomach reaches my mouth, and I almost vomit.

I can't dwell on my woe. I need the serum they've been working on. I take a breath and think. Where would it be?

05.05.1989 Final Test. The refrigerator.

A counter-height fridge is next to Dr. Petrovic's lab table. I pull open the door and on the top shelf is a row of syringes filled with that beautiful incandescent green slime. I grab one and race for the exit, but Dr. Petrovic enters, dragging the unconscious bald man with him. I skid to a halt, hiding the needle behind my back. I need to be smart, not tip my hand.

"What do you think?" Dr. Petrovic says, lifting his hair to reveal his skull, which looks like a rotting peach. He compares it to the bald man's. "Not a bad fit, eh?"

"You're going to chop off his head?"

"His head?" The doctor laughs and drops him to the floor. "Don't be absurd, Montague. Just his scalp."

This tops the crazy charts, even for Crampus. "What's happening to you?"

"Isn't it obvious? I'm decomposing, silly boy. Are you sure you're Robert's son?" He takes me by the shoulders, and I panic. He knows I've got serum behind my back. I waffle between stomping his foot or kicking him in the you-know-what, but it turns out he's just being the eccentric who invades your personal space. Pastrami breath and all.

"You see, since my original serum was taken from me,

I've only been able to create one with short-term results. Not ideal when experimenting on oneself, but when the university withdrew their support and removed my test subjects, what was I to do? Give up? Stop? Heed their threat of legal action? Fiddle-faddle!" Spittle hits my cheek, but I don't dare move. "I'll admit I was a tad shortsighted to compromise my own organs before I substantiated the efficacy of my new formula, but what's life without a few risks, eh? And now there's Houdini," he says with a wistful smile. "Proof that my original serum works. His cells hold the answer to longevity. He is the first step to immortality."

Immortality? "He's dying! His body is ice-cold, and he can barely breathe."

Dr. Petrovic's face turns to stone, and I realize he tricked me into admitting I have Houdini. He tightens his grip on my shoulders, thumbs digging into my pectorals. "Where is he?"

Schmelding enters, belching, and I use the distraction to ram Dr. Petrovic into him, sending them both toppling. I leap over them and out the door. My legs can't move fast enough to get me back to the lab where I left Houdini. I round the corner and—*wham!*—fly back like I was hit by a train.

It's Mr. Popsicle.

He reaches for me. I skitter away and run back around the corner, but hear Dad and Ashanta rambling frantically from inside the stairwell at the other end of the hall. I dive into a flimsy cardboard box as everyone emerges into this corridor at the same time: Dad and Ashanta from the stairwell, Mr. Popsicle from around the corner, and Dr. Petrovic and Schmelding from the lab. I can't let them see me, or I'll never be able to get back to Houdini without them following.

My hiding place is pathetic, but with all eyes on Mr. Popsicle, no one looks my way. The mutant breaks into a lumbering gallop toward Dr. Petrovic.

The doctor smiles, holding his hands to his heart proudly. "He's so beautif—"

Mr. Popsicle snatches him up by the neck, cutting him off.

Ashanta screams.

Dad jumps on Mr. Popsicle's back, trying to pull him off, and Schmelding draws his tranquilizer gun, looking for an opportunity to shoot.

Somehow Dad wrenches Mr. Popsicle's grip off Dr. Petrovic's neck, but the mutant slams against the wall, crushing Dad. Dad hits the ground.

Mr. Popsicle zeroes in on Dr. Petrovic again, but Schmelding fires. The dart lands in Mr. Popsicle's right butt cheek.

"Spiffy," Dr. Petrovic says.

Mr. Popsicle pulls the tranquilizer from his butt and jams it into Dr. Petrovic's head. The doc drops, groggy. Schmelding roars like a monster and takes aim again, but Mr. Popsicle snatches the gun from him and lodges a dart in his shoulder. Schmelding goes cross-eyed and drops. Mr. Popsicle turns to Dad now, foaming at the mouth, growling.

"Jeff," Ashanta says, getting his attention.

I brace for him to hurl her down the hall, but he doesn't. His face softens as he looks at her, like he recognizes her.

Tears stream down her cheeks, and she takes his hand. "I'm so sorry. I'm so sorry." She sobs now, the way Dad did when Mom died.

Jeff whimpers, and his grotesque mutations revert, like a movie in reverse, bringing him back to when he was normal. "Ashanta . . ." he whispers hoarsely and sinks to the floor. Dead, I think. For real.

She falls on his chest, grieving.

"Rats," Dr. Petrovic says, coming to, as he yanks the dart from his head. "Dead again."

The bald man stumbles out of the lab, woozy. "What . . . where . . ."

Dad whips his eyes to Dr. Petrovic, horrified. "Doctor."

The crazy doctor plays it nonchalant, inspecting his fingernails. "He's an organ donor. I checked his license."

Thunder!

Lights flicker.

Dr. Petrovic scurries off. "Gotta go. Split. Make tracks."

He disappears around the corner, but Dad remains in the hallway with the anguished Ashanta and the confused bald man, and I'm still trapped in this box when I need to get this serum to Houdini. I tear out of the cardboard, sprinting in the opposite direction. Dad shouts my name and footsteps chase me, but I'm well ahead of him.

To throw him off the scent, I bolt into the stairwell loudly so he hears me, then tramp up to the first floor and throw open the doors to the outside (as if I left), but instead, I hightail it down the corridor, around the corner, down that corridor around the next corner, and then quietly slip into the stairwell and tiptoe back down to the basement.

Just a few more minutes, Houdini. Just hang on a few more minutes.

CHAPTER 49

Houdini is stock-still.

I steady my emotional lips and put my ear to his chest to listen for a heartbeat. Faint, but there. "Hang on, Houdini. I'm here. I'm here."

With shaky hands, I uncap the needle containing the incandescent green slime. I've never given anyone a shot before. I pinch the skin on his scrawny shoulder until I have about half an inch of flesh to work with, and stab him before I lose my nerve. As I'm about the plunge the magic serum into him, behind me Dad yells, "Stop!"

Startled, I spin around, unintentionally ripping the needle out of Houdini's arm. The syringe is still brimming with the green slime. I didn't get a single drop in.

"Monty, that formula doesn't work," Dad says.

Ashanta's with him, and they're both ragged.

"What happened to Jeff, those mutations," she says, wiping her tear-swollen eyes. "That's what this serum does. We didn't know, but Dr. Petrovic has been doing his own tests. He dosed Jeff before the gala. You can't give it to Houdini."

"You're lying. Both of you. Liars!"

Dad looks like he's going to cry, and if he's going to cry, it's as bad as it gets. "I'm so sorry, Monty. I truly thought we could save him—"

"No! Don't say that."

The whine of an engine is upon us in an instant as Dr. Petrovic bursts in on his Vespa, nearly running down Dad and Ashanta. His passenger, Schmelding, jumps off as the doctor guns it. Toward me!

"Monty," Dad calls, but it all happens so fast I'm already flying through the air before it registers.

The doctor somehow managed to yank me off my feet and toss me away from Houdini. I hit the floor with a skid, but Dad scoops me up posthaste, and I'm airborne again. When my feet touch the ground, I'm shielded behind him. Schmelding points his tranquilizer gun at us, but the only thing that matters is getting back to Houdini. I wriggle out of Dad's grasp and make a run for it.

"Monty!" Dad calls.

Pht. Pht. Darts sail past my head. Schmelding's firing at me!

But it's Dr. Petrovic who stops me when he whips a syringe of green slime to Houdini's head. Ashanta shrieks. Dad does what he does—tries to defuse the situation with reason—but my focus is on that lunatic's thumb resting on the plunger. How can I get there before he pushes it?

"Ah, ah," he warns, as if he can read my mind. "Now, be a dear and leave. Everyone. Or the hairball gets it."

Schmelding about-faces for the exit.

"Not you, Schmelding," the doctor snaps.

"You said everyone."

The doctor sighs. "Everyone but Schmelding. Skedaddle."

"Why would you do this?" I ask, shaking my head. "You know it'll kill him."

"That formula was my brainchild, and he's all that's left of it. If I lose, we all lose. I'm not bluffing, Montague. I won't allow you to take what is rightfully mine."

"Please, Doctor Petrovic. He's my friend. I love him."

The doctor's eyes soften—the wonky one stops twitching—and then he turns to ice. "Boo hoo. Wah wah. I lost thirty years of research. That's decades. Every cell, tissue, and organ on this table belongs to me. And I will harvest all of it. The question is: dead or alive, Montague. Your choice."

A lump forms in my throat, suffocating me. I can't walk away from Houdini. I can't.

But I have to.

Numb, I turn to the only person who can understand my pain. "Dad . . ."

Dad wraps his arms around me, and I bury my face in his shirt. I've lost.

"Smart boy," the doctor says. "Go on, then. Scoot. Scurry. Scat. A living cell is better than a dead one."

"This isn't over," Dad says to Dr. Petrovic.

"Right you are, Robbie, Bobbie, Boo. This is merely the beginning."

A low, slow rumbling emanates, and we turn to Schmelding, thinking it's his stomach. He shrugs. "Ain't me."

CRACK! BOOM!

It's thunder.

The storm outside has picked up. An earsplitting roar shakes the building, and the fluorescent bulbs fizzle and crackle off and on. Everyone looks around as if they're waiting for the mother of all storms to hit, except me. I dive for the distracted Dr. Petrovic, grabbing his wrist and wrestling for the needle.

Schmelding aims his tranquilizer gun at me, but Dad tackles him to the ground.

Despite the doctor's rabid grappling, I twist his arm upward and thrust the needle in his mushy skull. Gasps from everyone except the shocked Dr. Petrovic.

"Drat" is all he says as he drops to his knees and face-plants to the floor. Bumps protrude from his skull, back, arms, and legs, turning him into a mutant like Mr. Popsicle. But just as quickly, they dissolve, and Dr. Petrovic stirs and mumbles incoherently.

WHAM! The door to the lab slams against the wall, startling all of us.

Dean Smith stands in the doorway with the security guard by his side. Shaking with rage, soaking wet from the downpour, Dean Smith marches over to the disoriented Dr. Petrovic. "You're fired. Tenure or not."

Half-dazed, the doctor doesn't put up a fight as he's hauled off by the security guard. Schmelding fakes right then left then right to get around the dean, who isn't trying to stop him, and scurries after.

"Make this disappear, Doctor Hyde, or the entire science department will." The dean about-faces and marches off.

I run to Houdini, scooping my emaciated friend into my arms. "Houdini?" He's unresponsive. "Houdini, please." I don't think he's breathing anymore. I turn to Dad, begging, "Do something. Help him."

"Monty, there's nothing I can do."

"No! How can this be? If love's not the answer and the serum's not the answer, then what is? There's gotta be something that will save him."

Dad looks at me, but doesn't need to say anything for me to know there is no answer.

Tears spill down my face. "So I'm supposed to just give up? Like you did with Mom?"

"Oh, Monty, is that what you think? I never gave up hope. Never. When you love someone you never give up."

"But they die anyway."

"Sometimes," he says on the verge of tears. "Sometimes there's nothing we can do."

"It's not fair!" I crumple onto Houdini's chest, crying. "It's not fair."

"I know, son." Dad rubs my back.

"What's the point of loving someone if they're just gonna die?"

"I wish I could tell you I had all the answers, but the truth is, I don't. It's why I took this job in the first place. Not because I thought I could bring your mother back, but because I was afraid of losing you or Kyle. I wanted to believe I could save you if the unthinkable happened. I wanted a guaranteed, foolproof way to stop you from dying. From leaving me."

I finally look up.

"But instead, I spent all this time worrying about losing you when I should've been cherishing the time I have with you now. I'm really sorry, Monty. I've been so consumed with my own pain and fear that I lost track of what's important. I was selfish, and I let you down when you needed me most. I hope you can forgive me."

My eyes are a stream, but I get it. If I thought there was a way I could've saved Mom or Houdini, I would've devoted every second of my life to it too. I nod. Of course I forgive him.

"Even though it hurts now," Dad says, "I think the point of loving someone is that no matter what happens, you'll always have the times you shared. You wouldn't want to give that up, would you?"

"No." I can't imagine not having had Mom or Houdini in my life. I wouldn't be me without them. I wipe my eyes and nose. "I'm sorry I was mean to you, Dad." I hug him for the first time in nearly two years. "I love you."

"I love you too, Monty."

Suddenly, a crackling rope of electrical energy shoots through the room, hitting all the equipment and sending everything haywire.

KA-BOOM!

The lights go out.

A radiant flash blinds me momentarily as a lightning bolt strikes Houdini in the chest.

"Houdini!"

I reach out, but Dad pulls me back. "Monty, don't, you'll electrocute yourself."

Houdini's veins glow beneath his skin. They're not coursing with blood, but with green slime. Slime that's bubbling, boiling, sizzling, like in Dr. Petrovic's experiment tape when the serum was hit with lightning.

After a moment, the fluorescents hum back to life, everything's calm and quiet, and smoke settles over Houdini.

"Houdini," I whisper, not knowing what to think. I take his open hand, clutching it tightly. It feels like he's holding mine back, but that can't be. Can it? My heart whirls with hope.

"Houdini?"

He blinks, opening his eyes, and mine instantly flood with tears.

"Houdini!" I throw my arms around him, and his featherlight arms hug me. My eyes are a river, and I sob loudly, but for the first time in a long time, I sob with happiness.

Dad and Ashanta mutter in disbelief with some tears of their own. Of course, they rattle off theories as to what might've happened, settling on the electrical current from the lightning restarting his heart like those paddles in the ER or in malls.

But it's obvious to me. Houdini never would've made it without love and magic tricks.

CHAPTER 50

A lot has changed in the three weeks since the gala.

Houdini's at full strength, a foot taller (at least one of us grew), and stinkier than ever. He still doesn't grasp that smelly is a bad thing, but I've gotten used to it. Like working in a fish shop. The good thing is I don't have to pretend I have diarrhea anymore to cover up his odor.

We also got proof that he wasn't eating anyone. Ever. I knew it, but Dad wasn't convinced until we found the missing students in the back of Schmelding's Animal Control truck. Alive. Fourteen in all, including Becky. Apparently, the wackadoodle doc was showering them with beer and nachos to get them to sign themselves over to his research.

Most surprising is the fact that I love living in a gated community now. With all the attention Houdini gets, it's nice to have security keep the lookie-loos out so we can have a normal life. Well, as normal as life can be with a monster. Frankly, that's the kind of thing that makes your house become the neighborhood hangout. And today's no different.

We burst through the door on our boards and sail off the

foyer into the living room. We being Ripper, Ella, Thrash, Chen, Houdini, and me. Ripper and I built a custom skateboard for Houdini, and FYI, he's a bit of a show-off.

Watson's smart enough to greet us with a wagging tail from the safety of the dining room, but Dad approaches, shushing us with his hand. He's on the phone. A chorus of "Sorry, Mr. Hyde," comes from my friends as we all leap off and catch our boards. All except Houdini, who ollies onto Dad's foot. Accidentally. The landing part, not the ollie part. Like I said, he's a bit of a show-off.

Grimacing, Dad manages to continue his call. "I'm flattered, and thank you again, but my family and I are very happy where we are."

That's the millionth job offer he's turned down since the fundraiser. Guess Houdini's not the only popular guy since the unveiling at the gala. Dad glares at me when he ends the call, as if I'm the one who trampled his foot. "Monty, what'd I say about skateboarding in the house?"

"I didn't know you were home."

He rolls his eyes, about to give me the what for, but Ashanta enters, and his face lights up, scolding forgotten. She's carrying four extra-large pepperoni pizzas—all for Houdini—which I grab before he mows her down.

"Thanks," I spit out and spin to halt Houdini with my stern look.

He hits the brakes, arms and legs flailing as he skitters, mostly in place. We really need to get some rugs. He manages a U-turn and scrambles into a seat at the table, salivating. Watson stands by his chair, staring at the floor for crumbs. Some things never change.

"I had a nice visit with Doctor Petrovic this morning," Ashanta says. "His psychiatrists are quite pleased with his progress. He rarely talks about robbing graves anymore."

"Just an ordinary day in Crampus," Ripper jokes. He's handling it pretty well, considering an aunt he never met moved here to take care of him.

"We'll be back around dinnertime," Dad says. He's going to a seminar with Ashanta (which is why I thought he wouldn't be here). "Don't fill up on pizza. It's for Houdini."

"Seriously? Have you not met him?" I motion to the table where four empty pizza boxes are all that's left. Poor Watson. Not even a morsel.

"Good," Dad says. "And I expect your homework to be done by the time I get back."

Amused, I snort. "As if."

Dad shoots me the look, and I scramble to cover. "As if I'd have it any other way."

"Know your audience, brah," Thrash says.

"Good advice," Dad chimes in.

I sigh.

"Later, skater." Ella's the first one out the door before Dad can kick them out.

Ripper, Thrash, and Chen hurry after, waving their goodbyes and saying things like, "Catch you on the flippity-flop, mop-top," and "Ciao for now, purple cow." Things we don't really say unless we're teasing each other.

"See you on the Nile, for a mile, crocodile," I throw back at them.

Dad grabs his coat. "Homework. Now." He kisses me on the forehead before I have the sense to duck.

"*Dad.*"

He chuckles and leaves with Ashanta.

House to myself, not counting Watson and Houdini, I break into a bag of Doritos Cool Ranch and a can of Sprite.

Both creatures hover over me, drooling, as I kick back on the couch and turn on the TV. "Not for you," I say, but they're laser focused on my snack. They don't even look over when Kyle and Diego enter.

"Homework, butt-wipe," Kyle says.

Crickets! Dad got to him. "I'm gonna do it."

"Yeah, you are."

"I know. I said so."

"I know you said so."

"Stop it."

"Stop what?"

"Doing that."

"Doing what?"

"Kyle!"

"Monty!"

Gaaagghhh. I toss the bag of chips at him and clomp my way to the stairs. Houdini and Watson battle for the lead, knocking me aside as they push their way through and race up. (Houdini's got the bag of chips. Don't ask.)

"Let me know if you need help," Kyle calls after. "Dad's not the only smart guy around here."

"Thanks, but I'm sure Diego has better things to do."

They laugh, and I continue up the stairs, glad Kyle has a friend like Diego. He lost a few with the whole skirt thing, but sometimes people just need time to realize that something they thought was a big deal, isn't. I have to give Dad credit, though. No one foresaw all these developments when we moved here. Especially the horrible things I said that I wish I could un-say. But Dad loves us, no matter what.

When I get to my room, Houdini is kicked back on my beanbag chair, which would be like me sitting on a hacky sack, but his choice. Watson is sprawled on my pillow. Another plus to dulling my olfactory senses: I barely notice the dog-butt odor when I go to sleep. And the Doritos bag is crumpled on the floor. Hopefully Watson got a taste, at least.

We're learning about body systems at school, and after everything I've been through, I can ace any test without cracking open a textbook, but homework counts for part of the grade. Problem is, I can't remember where I put my book.

I rummage through my backpack, my desk, my magic stand, and come up empty. I drop to the floor and sift through the junk under my bed, brushing aside dust bunnies, old shoeboxes, dirty dishes, and spot Ella's baseball cap. *Oh, yeah.* A smile plasters my face. I forgot I had it.

As I'm about to grab the cap, it twitches. I jolt back with a yelp so fast you'd think I was bitten by a snake. Watson and Houdini are on the floor pronto, flanking me. Together, we crawl slowly toward the bed and peer underneath.

Furry. Fuzzy. Wooly. Arms and legs sprouting out of the cap. Quietly, we stare. Until two eyes pop wide open.

"Agh!"

Watson scrambles back.

Houdini squeals with joy. *Squeeeee.*

But I clutch my heart, mind racing. Can it be? Is it? It has to be!

I peer under again. The most adorable Whopper-like eyes stare directly into mine and blink. *Dink. Dink.*

Oh, boy! Or girl? Who cares? I have another monster!

Wait. *I have another monster.* How am I going to convince Dad to let me keep another one in the house? *Hmm.* Maybe this should be our little secret for now.

ABOUT THE AUTHOR

Rhonda Smiley lives in Glendale, California, with her oft-writing partner, James Hereth, and their bossy dog, Jojo. She graduated from Concordia University in her native Montreal, Canada, with a major in film production, and has written for many shows, including *Ninja Turtles, Tarzan, Born Free, Kuu Kuu Harajuku,* and *Totally Spies!*

When not writing for television, she's tackling her own projects, like the animated feature *Race,* which she wrote and produced. In 2017, she released her first novel, *Asper,* for young adults who have a penchant for the darker side of fantasy.

Currently, she and James are working on their graphic novel, *Blowback.*

Monty and the Monster is her second novel.

Visit her @ rhondasmiley.com or @ blowbackuniverse.com

CPSIA information can be obtained
at www.ICGtesting.com
Printed in the USA
LVHW091627030920
665030LV00003B/427